I0749286

THE STORM

Also by John Fraser
and published by AESOP Modern Fiction:

Animal Tales
Behaving Well
Best Friends
Black Masks
Blue Light / Starting Over
The Beach
The Case
Confessions
The Cure
Down from the Stars
The Ends of the Earth
Enterprising Women
Exploring the Clouds
Fake Fur
FISH
The Future's Coming Everywhere
Happy Always
Hard Places
An Illusion of Sun
The Magnificent Wurlitzer
Medusa
Mercenaries
Military Roads
The Observatory
The Other Shore
Paradise
People You Will Never Meet
The Red Bird
The Red Tank
Runners
'S'
Short Lives
Sisters
Soft Landing
Strangers and Refugees
The Test
Thinking Scientifically
Thirty Years
Three Beauties
Tomorrow the Victory
True Stories
Unsteady States, Vols I and II
Wayfaring
Wisdom

THE STORM

JOHN FRASER

AESOP Modern Fiction
Oxford

AESOP Modern Fiction
An imprint of AESOP Publications
Martin Noble Editorial / AESOP
28a Abberbury Road, Oxford OX4 4ES, UK
www.aesopbooks.com

First edition published by AESOP Publications

www.johnfraserfiction.com

A catalogue record of this book is available from the British Library.

First edition 2012, revised 2014, 2020, 2024

ISBN: 978-0-9572061-0-6

PROLOGUE

CRAC

'WHEN DO you expire?' Goran asks Melinda: 'This anyway is just an exercise.'

The ministers cower down, like bats shaken from their hold, they're on the floor, broken crosses or immobile in a breast-stroke.

Grenades and crackers.

The fake emergency concludes. Melinda says, 'We're here to make them make the future. "To save the world" – how many times a conference on the theme? When this show is over, so's my contract. What can they expect?'

'The future ...' Goran says, and no doubt carries on, professional, authoritative and sceptical. I must make all this up. I'm in a box, buried shallow in a field, my last gasps coming through a straw.

The guys will dig me up if someone pays a ransom. Maybe they'll dig me up if no one pays, and they've no cash to make a getaway. Maybe they won't dig me up.

HAIL, HAIL, the powerful of the earth! And – Hail too the tempest, hail to the four horsemen! Compose, propose, dispose! Defend, defend – here comes the end.'

Valhalla trembles – but we're all still here – one end has come, but others wait, and we're to be the witnesses.

The set of trumpeters steps up. A blast.

Up turn the faces, hopeful. Nothing. Just – up where the sky should be.

We three are called to a conference. On the floor, the big guys, making futures and a florid past. We write the policies – Melinda for a hot, middling, rising place. A land where pineapples bloom disciplined, in line. Goran's from a shady place, working for shady people. My country is quite desperate, recovering from war to make the next one.

Melinda says, 'It's not a fake, a plastic cheeseboard, with its map and flags. Like well-off people used to have, with pictures of each cheese. These guys – the leaders of the world – they're just the middling cheeses, some ripe, that's hung on for years, and cling till death. There is no super kingly Parmesan. There's creamy ones, elected and ephemeral. Newly pressed, first salting. How the people despise, distrust them all – the seasoned despots and the runny ones, the bland and milky ones, the crusty stinky ones.'

Goran says, ‘Up on the catwalk – here you see everything.’

Down there, what a spread! You see the heads, but not the mouths, the brains. Those must be Jews or cardinals in skullcaps. The rich in white, like sellers of ice-cream. Africans in stuff that could be curtains. The structure, the hall – like the rail station in Istanbul, iron fingers curved above; below, the tracks that ought to go to China.

Up here, there’s parakeets and jays – ‘We love the birds,’ Melinda says. ‘Because their eyes see just the same as us, but out it comes all different, you can’t say it’s fantasy or manner – it’s just difference.’ And we agree.

What a congress! So many countries – there’s one fallen! in the crush, picked up and swallowed down – ‘That’s the pope,’ Melinda cries, but no, it’s just some nurse’s cap she sees, – and here’s the suits from way out East, they nod and bob to all the guys that owe them scrip.

‘Here come the drinks,’ Melinda says. ‘That shows who has teetotal gods, and who’s for health,’ and round it goes – the scotch, the brews of leaves.

‘Help me, o rescue me,’ says Goran. ‘What shall we do in our hereafter?’

Melinda smiles, and does not know.

Goran tells her, 'Bits of you I like, very much.' He thinks – 'They'd never take me, as a guard. I haven't the fibre. Imagine, prisoners, and snow and trees.'

Not necessarily trees.... He goes on, 'And the people locked in – suppose there was an innocent, and all your time to think what you might be guilty of. Innocence – it's just perspective, and guilt is just the same. We guards – knowing who to trust, and living in some hole, for warmth, and getting up before the rest to take roll call.'

Melinda has said, 'I see it wouldn't be for you.'

Goran has said, 'I'm just not up to it.'

Melinda says, 'I've suffered too. Not alcoholism, not like you, Goran, nor thinking of the prison service. It's enough our lives make sense to us, not in the world. Think of them as beautiful.'

'You can't ruin my life,' Goran says, 'It's ruined like the rest. What's left is – the gaze, of others. You can't escape. What you want to do with other people? Kill them in the cellar?'

'Not specially,' Melinda says, dismissively.

'So, we just walk on, walk away,' says Goran, 'Forget about the sense.'

Yes, there should be a romance here – beyond the countries, the position papers and all that, world's end, and how to interrupt the process.

Now, they're joined by Mister Kite, a colleague older, better contract, almost a diplomat. He says,

'Ah yes – if only there was a clash that you could see, a battle, conflict, struggle. But, my friends, I fear big changes go ahead quite tranquilly. From crawl to walk: from hunt to plant. Of course, some things you notice, you'd be stupid not to. New rich guys – up on the podium. Sects, principles, the dangers imminent – even new animals, strange crops, stuff hidden in the ground. And so, you guys, you're civilised, you write it up – 'here comes the transformation!' – but fight! Do battle? Fight personal? You wouldn't dream of it, and you'd be right.'

'What's new,' Melinda says, 'Comes like a gift. You play it right, and you are bonded in. You must become a vassal of the new, the new rich guy. Protection – you need it, that way you're not extinguished.'

'It's not so,' Goran says. 'It's the thought that counts, puts asphalt on the roads, swings in the playground, sets the guys marching up the hill and through the desert. Thought first – then perhaps your submission, for the gift.'

'Well, why does it not go on and on, renewal? Why does it falter, why do some guys deride, while others wave their arms and run to battle?' asks Mister Kite.

'Maybe there is no choice,' says Goran, and Kite says that's no answer. They close him out.

'It's liberal rhetoric, all of it,' says Goran, 'Or something partisan.'

'Yet it's natural that you believe it's getting worse, or better,' Melinda says.

'Should we go in to dinner together? Is it time?' asks Goran.

'No, it's coming up to lunch – we might renounce lunch, in solidarity, as a sacrifice. Dinner was yesterday. And you go in separately, or they think it is a plot,' Melinda says.

'It's good being up high,' says Goran.

'You see into unsavoury rooms,' says Melinda.

'That's not what I mean,' he says.

They digress. 'It takes a thousand people to turn a graphic novel into film,' she says.

'The boxes are all ready-drawn,' says Goran, 'The rest is up to you.'

She says, 'The movie has no box, it's all to be scratched on, or stewed.'

'Then, you must think "box-office" – no joke there,' he says. 'The movie is all one piece, but it takes a mind to make it make a sense, to share a mood. Then there's the ads – laid out like cartons in the store: the thought becomes an object and you take it home. If you've the cash,'

'There's revolution too – that's a movie guys will try to copy,' says Melinda. 'So, the trick's the same. Making sense – that is the action. Movies have it, graphics don't.'

'It's not turned out at all like that,' says Goran, 'And the cash is not relevant. One day, one box – that is the trick. Analysis, not flux.'

'All those dead, to commemorate,' she says. There is exhortation everywhere – and the dying, hunger, war, all round.

'War, what do you expect?' asks Goran: 'Those machines; the tough guys enrolled and scared.'

'Maybe I could give some testimony,' she says.

'You need to rough up somewhat – now, you're too exquisite,' Goran says.

Melinda is Cuban, so Goran says, 'I've always been a communist. It's our only hope.'

She waits for something more. He says, 'Of course, not everything: consider details. The outcome, maybe, or not. Things going wrong.'

Cuba's not her country now, of course. There is a pause, she says, 'It's abstractions. They're a deep pit. You need to scrabble to get out of them.'

She shows him photos: there's a line of glum people with red knees. Tourists: 'A pineapple farm.'

'What's they come to see?' Goran asks, without enthusiasm.

'Pineapples, mostly,' she says. 'Then they go away with one. Mostly they throw them in the bushes.'

She asks, 'What'll you do in life, Goran? It can't be only solitude. And let it be far from me; you are – too noisy in the night.' She thinks, too, who'd fantasise about some ugly person?

Goran says, 'It's the drink. It struggles to get out, to reach a top. You see – each box, it has its logic, but one after another, things make a story, make a narrative. It doesn't take a thousand people to have it make sense, but together with the frames that follow in an order, inexorable and for ever – that is the sense. Slow and sure.'

Melinda objects – 'But it's not my sense, not this disjoint. Our conference – another in the chain to save the world – and in the end, someone will know how it worked out. But you and I – we will be unemployed. Now the big ones think of splitting up – America, there's mountains, rivers, sea and deserts – each a little unity. And China – wow! – there's seven good-sized units there, and each a perfect size. Then – after, what will life be for you, Goran?'

'I'll mostly work at home,' he says, to make her angry.

'Justice,' Goran says. 'Now, there's a precious gift. A thing you may resent, giving it out, when you'd prefer to keep it for yourself. But – there it goes! – a gift you can't get back. Me – I think revenge is more a human thing.'

Melinda agrees, 'Not everyone likes what they're given.' He says,

'It's what we all deserve, they say. You can't object, you get what you deserve. That's only fair.'

'These systems here, it must fit in with them.' Melinda waves around, the delegates, the bosses.

'These monsters,' Goran says, 'We'll strip them down, and of the parts assemble new ones. New sets of monsters, all recycled, new models all.'

In my box, all underground, I think – up there, sounds of a storm, insistent scratchy animal, a porcupine against the doors, those darts – or something tweaked by humans into fearsomeness – a leogryph, perhaps, that's after you, wings of an eagle, body of a lion, and beak of parrot – is this the noise it makes? What might it eat? It pounces on you, down you go: and then, a peck.

Knock knock – the old fool king, blinded, betrayed – don't let him in, his terrible back story, assassins too, though they don't knock ... the dopey prince, clubbing again, and clubbed with pills – don't let him go downstairs, let in the magic wind, force open closets, billow the hangings, flunkeys disclosed, cowering and probably disloyal. I think, quite desperate–

'It's just the wind. No one is there. Stop this panic. Wind in your ears. Just nature. Try a sleep? Sleep too has its troubled history ...'

Quiet. You're buried. And you can't hallucinate – just panic. Bury some bastard criminals yourself, and leave them ... little headstones – 'crime didn't pay'.

Melinda says, 'Of course, Goran, most things are revenge, but no one says as much. I'd like to help you,' but he goes on,

'You can have capitalism, or you have the state, but we, everyone, has got them both. That makes a lot of rules.' Melinda says,

'You have to take a chance. You need help or courage, if you want to trash stuff and people too,' and Goran says she hasn't understood, not peace nor battles make a difference at all. That is the nub. 'The end's inscrutable, beginnings have long gone,' he says.

Melinda has no answer, naturally. She says, turning all her sides, an invite to him, 'I could quite well be a tragic heroine. After all, what does it take?'

'Pathos and a bad end,' Goran says.

'The people here, they make me frightened. Can they really keep the fire and water out?' she implores. Rhetorically.

'We did it at school,' says Goran: 'Dialectics. Conflict, compromise, and pouf! Sometimes pouf, conflict, pouf! They didn't tell you it all, nor how long the stages last. I preferred the royal burials – when they got rid of the fancy stuff, the jewels, and good riddance, and the slaves and horses too. There's a lesson! You're wrong, to think I'd be angry at the end of the world. Blame, revenge – it would be childish.'

Melinda says, 'You're short on wonder, Goran.'

He says, 'They still quarrel over who we are, we Macedonians. Greeks, slaves, primitives. At times I feel I'm Turkish – or Bulgarian. It's quite a joke. The big thing is having royals buried near your home.'

'That music must be French,' says Goran. 'It's about going to the stars. Remember those fifties' ceiling lights? White glare?'

'At least in music, you get to make a noise. Though it does irk, those slow passages you must sit through,' Melinda says.

'If you're the composer, you get to go to the concert. All those people. Drinks. If you write a book, you never see who's reading it. No one ever finishes, gets to the end,' says Goran: 'Trains – that's the thing – German trains – on time, and no one steals your case. Stuff the words into your head, silent. Mulch. A book read to its end, exhausted and decanted. Emptied out.'

Suddenly he says, 'This conference – it's certainly a dud. We shall all die, soon. And suffer, angry. It won't be silent, like those guys who made a corporation, killing prisoners of war. Quick and easy. But all these crap guys here, they'll all go down, all the servants, civil or mostly not. No one here marched, or planned. But they sure plot a lot.'

'Poor food!' says Melinda, 'Yum yum, my favourite! *Frites*, and that red acid sauce,' and she eats them: 'It would be worth it, being poor, if you could live on these.'

'It looks like it will end,' says Goran. 'I smell the open sea, freedom. Nietzsche, our great master, called it that. What do you need to float on it – a plank? A liner? – that, he didn't say. Meanwhile, we wait, it's better to be rich. Let your slogan be – 'Forego the *frites*'. These guys here,' and he points down to the conference floor, the turmoil, guys with their plastic forks and red sauce down their face and shirt, 'They just skim off. The real cash isn't here – there's just a line of zeroes on a pad, a digit at the front, like Alexander's army, sweeping all away, then building new towns on the old. Homesick, or disappeared.'

A pause.

'Nice skin,' says Goran, patting Melinda's, 'Goes all round, and inside too, probably. A complete job.'

'That doesn't adhere,' Melinda says, 'Your observation, that is.'

'Your pathos,' Goran says, trying to stir some skin. 'Your pathos – it is touching. Your red pants, all those clothes, lying vulnerable and sullen, waiting to be put on, on someone in a hurry, naked and vulnerable. For what? To serve this cauldron of beings? All these surfaces, the skins, the suits – even to make a picture of it all that makes some sense ... Complicated, extensive, trivial too, the structures, relationships, hoisted up, like ants lifting twigs. Your analysis goes wrong and pouf! – you're fired, swept away – there's always more pouf to hand. Just your pathos stays, I see your pug face, closed – it speaks of sadness. These bad guys – they want to suck you in, it's crap, they suck your bones and spit the juice. Your skin though – stretches like a shoreline – here's the firm, and over there's the fluid.'

'Forget this skin approach,' Melinda says: 'I'm not impressed.'

'Here's the animator,' says Melinda, pleased to be done with courtship, quite unwanted. The leaders stomp on, dressed in sheets. She says, 'First there were darts, then board games – you imagine how those ended. Now, to keep them happy – it's theatricals.'

The guys have long ash poles, and beards. A chorus, somewhat Greek, They shout, 'koax koax, green are our bellies and yellow our backs.'

They are serious and passionate. 'They've never seen a frog,' Melinda says: 'They're waiting for someone, someone from the sea.... Saviour, avenger, liberator, too. But the chorus never suffers. At the end, just wrings its hands – and your heart.'

'Helen? Is she in this?' asks Goran, 'Is it that kind of play?'

'Elsewhere, screwing or tricking. This must be the version where the war comes at the end – the hero, sailor, hasn't left a war, he's seeking one. Odysseus coming home, shoots down some generals,' Melinda says.

'It sounds perfunctory,' Goran says, abstractedly.

'They like to chant, before the carnage,' Melinda says.

'Goran,' says Melinda kindly, resting her body on him, 'About the skin approach. Just ask a girl if she wants a date, a bedding down. They appreciate it – straight. Move with the clock, my dear. Courting is fine, it's just – it wastes the time.'

'All right,' says Goran hopefully: 'A date, Melinda? At my expense.'

'Not a hope,' Melinda says: 'It's not because you're squat and beetly – the blacksmith type – it's just – I can't stand being bored ... watching the sea, for sailors coming from their quest, to start a war.'

'These guys,' says Goran, 'We bring them all together, have them drink and play. Put on their actors' boots, and wigs and paint. Be friends. Bring gifts. Talk over – judge, assassinate, bombard, subvert, defame or ridicule. Expunge or cleanse, deport and jail and spy. Redraw the boundaries, and modernise and dig for gold, redraw the maps and block the river, build the dam so high, and classify – by sex and age and race and health and faith, intelligence or muscle-power ...'

'Yes, yes,' Melinda says, 'I know the job, these guys, they come and go, so what's your point?'

'The moral purpose,' Goran says, 'It's all around and no one sees. Goodness. It is said to be an end. In itself, with no reward, no delegation – just you and it.'

'Then there's the innocent, and victims,' Melinda says, and Goran says,

'No, no, those have their innocence and impotence – let them enjoy it if they can. It's goodness that should count – not the saving of the world. The being good.'

'This being in the world,' Melinda says, 'It suits me, never felt better.'

Goran agrees, but, 'This conference money that they pay – you can only spend it when there's other conferences.'

Melinda ignores him: 'Look at the chorus – their faces all floured up. There's France! Those swarthy short guys, how they love the stage. Quite bizarre. And those stick-like ones – can't get their mouths around the Greek.'

The countries wheel around and chant: 'The gods, the gods, are whipping up a storm – see the tin roofs, fly off like carpets, and – o my, the twisters, bear you up and smash you down, o sailor boy.'

'I didn't know this was a play – I thought it was in graphics,' Goran says: 'Anyway, what was the point, the sailor?'

'He couldn't sail a paper cup,' says Melinda assuredly: 'He was a warrior. The point was, to do the killing and so end the tale. That's all there ever is, in journeying. You make it or you don't. It's still a journey, only.'

*

I have arrived.

'I'm late,' I say. 'I bet this skirmish escalates.'

'Your country's down there, mouthing out, a big stick and pizza paste all over,' Melinda says.

The chorus in antiphony shouts out – 'A wreck! We're foundering!' and the others, 'Here's the pigs, swum out to save us.'

I ask, 'What's this crap?'

'Why are you late?' asks Goran: 'And you're not our sailor. Saviour. Not by half.'

I say, 'A guy – he said he knew me. I got into his car. They kidnapped me, and then they buried me. In a field. In a box. With a straw to breathe through, and hope, yes, always hope, no goat sat on my spout.'

*

'That's quite dramatic, if it's true,' says Melinda: 'It's clear it didn't end as you think it might.' I say,

'They called some numbers for a ransom. No one answered, so they dug me up. Forget the logic of it – but sheer humanity won through. Must be some American philosophy – what luck they weren't Spinozans, those guys couldn't care less what happens to you. It's that gap between truth and meaning – "Mind the gap", they used to shout, those guys. How wise, how true! Wise at least: – "between the train and the platform". That's how it is, the train that moves – meaning. Truth is the platform, where we stand ... Of course, if ransom's paid, they might well leave you there. It may sound pompous, but down there in the box, all around the earthy creatures, – who knows what they do? – and things put down there, hidden for eternal loss – I felt at one with all mankind. The world, the end – and will they dig you up? Spade in extremis? Or leave you there, and no one knows?'

It was a lie – I didn't think of kings, mankind, the earth, or any goddam thing. Just panic, breathe and suffer like a toad.

'No profit, no murder,' says Goran: 'It sounds admirable. All has had its reward.'

*

They soon forget my drama. Goran says, 'The play, the life, it's about journeys, not people. Of course. Look at the petrol wars. And history – it's about leaving Africa, finding horses, and then breeding better ones.'

'No horses in Africa,' Melinda says, keen to agree and press along. 'That's why they use drums. Communication.'

'No drums in the Andes,' Goran says. 'Or horses.'

'That's why there's confusion about human sacrifice,' she says: 'I hear there's war again – lines in the sand. I bet they send you, Goran; sort it out. Our guys here are restless, want their photos taken, then off home. They're not supposed to say they want a war, whatever they might feel.'

'And that is right,' says Goran. 'That leaves space for us. We're not in service, so we can say – 'put things back, just as they were'. Of course,' he laughs. 'The best thing for everyone is horns and fawns – a ballet company, for every nation. All need one – small theatres and free seats.'

'I didn't know that side of you,' Melinda says, impressed, 'The people that we know, they laugh at talk of dance – and not to mention poetry and such,' and Goran says,

'We left the dance behind, when we came out of Africa. It's all a twist of memory, what we have now, is just the mathematics of it. Stroking and twirling in the gym.'

Goran seems from the earth, himself, from digging, hammering – wiping his dark face with black hands. You'd give him temporary jobs, the dangerous ones, and send him back to rock and fire, to make your horseshoe or your goad.

'Now you know you won't have me,' Melinda asks him, 'How far would you go ...?'

'For love? For what I can't have? For anything? Quite far,' he says.

'O yes?' she says. 'You're sure? You've checked your wheels and cogs, your – what you run on? Gas?'

'Steam,' says Goran: 'Water you can always find. The sea! The sea!'

'I like determined guys,' she says. 'But not just obstinate.'

'Old plays had epilogues,' says Goran, looking down: the play without a plot, just happening. 'It was reassuring then. You need starts and finishes.'

'Well,' I say. 'We're all being finished. Our contracts end, and then we're free. Our countries will go on, I guess.'

'The bigger the things they're asked to do,' says Melinda. 'Be sure the least gets done.'

There's a clatter, as the chorus throw their poles – now it's high-kicking, arms linked behind, eyes bulging, sweat mixes with the flour and fard.

'There's my country, my boss,' says Goran, and he points: 'The others bear him up. He kicks, he pulls them down. It's a transition. No heroics.'

'My boss – is that big one, the old tart,' Melinda says: 'After the adieu photo, I'll find a bigger cheese and be his moll.'

'Desertion. They chop your fingers off, before the acid makes you disappear,' says Goran. 'It's all strategy, not sides. The great thing is – have your good time, before the music ends.

'Forget about good guys – there's no clause for them. Fry or starve, that is the story, and its end. This conference will make your flesh crisp up.'

'It's been the end of the world, ever since the start. People can't wait – or else they want to be the last, not wanting it going on without them,' Melinda says.

'When we've done,' says Goran, 'I'll go into the part of entertainments where you wear your clothes. Fired from cannons, maybe.'

'You're right,' Melinda says. 'Don't shed your threads – even, have them make a uniform.'

'I feel I could be a revolutionary,' Goran says. 'Or at least think in a revolutionary way.'

I say, 'That second way will keep you out of jail,' and Melinda adds, 'And let you choose your friends. But, Goran, on the whole, and you having an unappetising look – being fired from cannons – probably, that's your best shot.'

I think, then say, 'My soul is in that box, down in a shallow underground. How shall I get it back?'

'It may be best for you,' she says. 'To leave it. Do without it for a while,' and Goran nods – 'These guys,' he says, and gestures down, the guys, their countries, in a mill below. 'Each shines upon his turf, it's when they're all together that you see – we haven't got a hope, we're going down,' and then he says how elephants have always crossed the mountains, that's their best trick, walking to India and back – that too would be 'tough deal' if there'd been nothing in between but sand and soldiers, but there were farms and cities all the way, with figs and melons, cities of mud and towns of stone, princesses of filigree, pet storks that draw with pens.

'I'm with Phoenicia,' he says. 'And I'm against the Macedonians, though they were my fathers – ate everything before them, the shining fruit, and left that grim imperial style,' and Melinda acts provoked. The argument goes on.

*

'There should be some heroes, a big actor, make the speech,' says Goran. 'But here they just read out a prompt.'

The chorus marshals up, falls into silence, into rows. A leader is pushed forward, and he says,

'We are agreed. The world – it will not end. Should it insist, "its death, or ours" – we'll find a way to make it last,' and Goran says,

'The Trojan war – that didn't happen too. I saw the play.' Melinda says to hush him, how a Chinese guy says it's all cosmology, he has no picture of a world that ends, it can't be drawn, it's boring, but the world just goes on and on, 'it gyres around a point, is all' – and other guys applaud or smirk or sneer; and Goran says quite loud,

'That's it. Our contracts have expired. We gave our views, our expert thought – and now we're off and out, the party's done, and so ...'

*

'There's something at the gates,' she says.

So there is.

Not magic, not monster, not a tiger, but close to these: a storm of something. Nature.

I was saying 'Left and right, good and evil, yes, that's pretty much as it is, it was, and should be,' and I hear Goran. 'The blood on my doorstep's fresh – it didn't quite creep underneath my door, but it's waiting there, war and what they call armed struggle, deplorable, but not quite negative,' and Melinda musing, 'Finding direction, what my friends, my youth proposed, and for a while it seems, postponed...'

Then in it bursts. It takes some arms and swirls, a leg, and twists. O no! There go the heads, like on matchsticks in a box spilled out, and dancing through the walls that fall apart, the back wall goes as if it's never been. Curtain up, behold a troubled landscape. Off with them all, all proud, the tough, the wheedlers, those with crests engorged – they're seized and down they go, and out – as if they had the plague, chased out anonymously. There go the tags, the names, there's Poland – you can just read '-land', and there go other 'lands', republics whirling off, popular and not, faithful maybe, the king and queen – 'doms' go down, the houses, royal and not. And now here comes the stuff they promised us, sailing on the tide, away, away, the radios, retreaded tyres, patched, worn – dancing, gyring, but so purposeful ...

'It's air! It's water!' Melinda shouts, and adds, 'We're safe up here – but there they go, the heroes, leaders,' and she turns to me, 'You brought this on – you! sailor from the sea, you should have stayed down there, stuffed in your wooden box, a submarine that's ceased to float, you lie there stiff and calm – they say that at the end, you get euphoria,' and Goran says,

'They say, they say – how do they know? The guys that know, they've all been swept away, and all their houses after them, the limousines as well,' and on he goes, it seems it's time to think and not to say – although Melinda says, 'We're safe, above it all, the structure bends but does not snap,' but then you think, o no, there's all the after, consequence, some of it already here, and so I say,

'We'd better find a vehicle that takes us far away, there's too much nature here – it sometimes spared the sheep and goats, but this is quite too much. Those guys may try to find a landfall, island full of beasts that sing their warriors' song and chase them round, but nature's won the war and it will lick their bones.'

Melinda says, 'Poor guys,' but I do not.

The hall is full now; the people have been swept and brushed away. The place is full of spume, a fluid charged with nothing, heavy with recoils, the counterblows of gross things lifted off, in flight.

'It's quite portentous, this,' Melinda says. 'We talked for days of how it might not end, our world, and now – full stop, for all those guys. Catastrophe, and loads of junk, all broken up ...' She'd like to say 'poor guys' again, it sounds too weak, and Goran says,

'Just people, gone and going, as they do. What is this milky turbulence that's left – was it their wanting things, and mostly for themselves, but wanting it so much it was electric, like when the wires have gone: a broth of longing, to be great, remembered, words pinned on swelling breasts...?' How trite. He says, 'I'd love to see tomorrow's papers!'

So we shall.

'It's not a proper flood,' I say, 'Just a catastrophe, millions of miraculous escapes, guys found to fill the gaps, and no one chastened much.'

'Our work,' says Goran. 'All that paper. Waste. No use now. Just literature.'

'Should we be feeling freer now?' Melinda wonders, and Goran says there's always contracts, our word, that didn't quite expire with all those leaders swept away:

'What they should do, having the chance,' he says, 'is set new countries up, redraw the boundaries. Put spells on all the islands, votes for pigs and penguins, and for monsters too, promote enchantresses, obey the oracles. And every while, we'll swirl them all around, our lucky few, survivors – the mountaineers will plod the deserts, river folk will make the cheese,' and on he goes. Melinda says,

'The problems, Goran! Problems! How they're going to solve, forever on the move?'

He says, 'That's rubbish! You never solve the problems – just look for the bits of pleasure lying in a scatter round about. The problems come from staying still and digging holes and making ramparts, forging steel and planting trees – of course that way the guys will fight for territory, and all the stuff they've found, and churches too and burials with sacrifice, and aeroplanes, and going here and there and on the cheap and hurrying back, and "here's the peak of culture", "there's a pole to dance around, and make the river flow uphill, and pull that ugly mountain down, and eat those mouflons' eyes and throw the rest away"...'

'Yes, yes,' Melinda says. 'We know all that – it's order, rules, that matter, if we move around or if we wait our turn to starve or fry,' and Goran says that's why they paid us, write a policy, ferment it, and all turns into literature, and so he laughs and laughs. 'The answer is to be a god, ride out the storms,' and then he says, 'But no – there's always bigger gods, they screw the little ones and turn them into eucalyptus trees.'

If Goran were a god, he'd be underground, to hammer out those brittle swords and spears.

We come to terms with it, what comes next.

'I've seen Goran's girl,' Melinda says, 'She's fifteen. She wears go-go boots and drinks vinjak.'

'She sounds speedy,' I say.

Melinda's angry, and she shouts at me, 'You post-colonial tarts! Doing the round of fractured peoples, who can't trust their own. You – expert of nothing, for hire, forever.'

'Yes,' I say, 'That's exactly it,' and she's angrier still. I say, 'It's the world, Melinda, if you ignore it, you'll fall off.'

'I only think about the future,' Melinda says, primly, 'I'm not sure that Goran does. Or you.'

'Just think of all of us, happy and stateless,' I say – but of course, she's not, not yet, she has some ties – this middling state, its middling loyalties.

'It's all to do with people,' she says. 'People below, elected ones above. All people, just so. Constantly regenerated. We sound a trumpet, now and then, or wave a standard. We're with them, everyone.'

I say, 'Melinda – you're crazy. Making things up.'

'The half that I make up,' Melinda says, 'About how it works, the loyalty and such, fits with the half, the other half, that you invent.'

'No,' I say. 'I don't have time for that. You think there is a wisdom somewhere, blowing it along, a salty sailor wrecked who crawls ashore to take you back to wholesome lands. It isn't so – he'll croak on landing, or he'll be another mouth, another pair of meddling hands. Skilful with knots – and there you have no rope.'

Melinda talks on – it starts with go-go boots, and – how she gossips through! – and where's she want to end? To sail away from this poor land, its trees and buildings meshed and strangled up – the three of us, for company, then each with a different province, hers doing best, and people being grateful or ignored. I say,

'Melinda, people must find it hard to swallow you.'

'Things go on, you know,' Melinda says, expansively, turning away from what the storms had left: 'Change. Up and down. God. Winters. The communists, those guys, said it could all be steadied down, with sharing. Everyone dealt identical hands. Well, what a joke! That fell through – a hundred years ago, it seems, and now you,' she points at me. 'You can't think of anything at all – not something better, not something worse. You crouch around that emptying cooking pot. Goran's more enterprising – when his girl grows up, he'll find some more, and younger still – at least he knows they'll all grow up and leave. Without regrets.'

'Or with regrets,' I say. 'But then, who cares?' – anxious to cut her short, this trite relations stuff – it seems to suit her, but I'd rather talk about my box. Now, there was closure!

'To get on,' Goran says, 'you need a memory of at least a thousand years. Then, a brief revolution and a famine. Melinda doesn't have all that – but beneath the snob, there is her ordinariness, so clean and crafty ... She know the rules, and so how they are broken.'

Long ago, the days of innocence:

Melinda, when first I saw her, was a street singer, of the highest class. Put a toe in the arts, you end up in the rain, on a corner, a twisted familiar with a drum, crouched by your knee, and looking up at you.

'Ignore this guy, I can't get rid of him,' but then he rattles off his rataplan – here comes the scornful crowd!

She sings, 'These brilliant days, so crisp, chocolate and rose – how shall we remember them, my love? Last days – I hear the distant wind ...'

How beautiful she is. That's why they took her on the singing course.

'There's your usual ungenerous thought,' says the stunted drummer: 'I know you.' 'Definitely not,' I say, 'I don't know you – just the singer, only.'

'She represents a country – when she doesn't sing, of course – about the size of France,' he says: 'Beauty may come into it – the singing, though, is just spare time.'

Melinda says, 'This inappropriate guy – I don't know him, or either of you two.'

‘Women sing, men drum,’ says the drummer wisely. ‘That’s the way it is now,’ and Melinda says, yes, and women die and men are tortured, that’s the new way too, and on she sings, like all my women have, and maybe that means she’ll be one of them, but – ‘O no,’ Melinda says, ‘My middling country, with its villages and goats – no, I can’t let you in,’ and she raises up a foot against me, like a parade horse, to show it’s legs and sex she’s guardian of, and all that stuff ephemeral, as she’s a centre of profoundest thoughts.

She sings, *I sought the desert, for my life was full of trivial things –*
In the sand, the flowers bloom once a century –
see them, like jewels, the yellow pink and blue –
I sought a desert, o my love, the desert – it was you ...
and on she goes.

‘Here comes some guy,’ the drummer says, and here he is, dark stooped, a woolly cap, a vacant look, loping along – ‘You’ll see, he’ll drop some tin,’ and up he comes, a-jingle of his coins. And in the cup they go.

‘Hi, Melinda,’ says the guy. The disguise – a pretend: it’s just a prank....

She pats his head, and sings.

*

'This guy,' the drummer says. 'He used to have a motor, furry dice and love-lights – only one in town. Now he's an expert, and they pay him for his stories of the sorry place he comes from. Hi! Goran!'

'Watch this guy,' Goran tells me, joshing round. 'He'll sell you to a gang.'

Just to make some noise, I say, 'I know all about singing,' but the drummer insists, and says,

'Then, Goran, the little tricks got bigger, and you lost the car and all the rest, and had to hide the past ...' Goran interrupts, he says the past deserved it, some guys have a past that's gold and diamonds, that's for sure, and let them put it in a casket, rejoice – and on he goes, a proof of honesty is losing everything and been found out. The drummer says Melinda learned her trades by being kept and having someone pay for her – except she never learned what 'being kept' involved. She laughs and says, 'Love? Just when it's all died off? Singing's harder than some trills of sex that isn't worth a speck of gold, nor diamonds too ...' and she is right. What keeps us vertical is shoes and boots, and evolution too.

The drummer makes his rataplan, and skitters up and down, the crowd dissolves, some guys have found some foreign coins and leave them in the cup.

Now:

Goran says, 'They haven't got new leaders picked, not yet, there's only us, the experts, left. Those guys, our mates, that represent much land mass' – and he spreads his arms, to left, to right, they're wings of Habsburg eagles, and he makes as if he's got two heads – a beak to east, to west: 'They think of making pacts. Russia and China – the problem is the shamans in between,' – it seems there's deadlock, and the shamans know what's underground, from going down to hell and such, and totting up reserves, the rocky stuff down there. And then America and India – both with Indians all over – they'd get together, but there's Arabs in between. And so we think what we three might do, re-drawing boundaries and finding friends – and should we look for modest lands to settle in, with people, or start off somewhere, just us three, avoiding citizens and subjects, stuff in the subsoil, tides and mountains too...?

'Come on!' says Goran, 'I'm not a Han, and nor are you, and maybe China's always been the species-hope, but do you care about all that? That wavy thing, disaster – call it catastrophe – that swept the big and little cheeses out the back wall – that's just an episode. Higher and higher go the castle walls, and mister Capital, the newest god, perches atop them, invisible, ineffable – weightless it seems, but oh! the walls, they crumble. He remains aloft, a sack of sacred air. And we shall be the first to go. Atonement. Sacrifices. So – let's make a "bloc anomalous". Melinda, her country is the size of France, and mine is not, and yours' – he points to me – 'is just late come-by. Then there's the Arabs, desperate and feisty too – we'll put them all together, not leave them scattered all about ... Resist!'

'But if it's unavailing, Goran? We're the experts, it is true, we all come from the streets ...' I say. Melinda says, 'I don't. I've landed in the street, is all, spare time,' and so we stare around.

The drummer makes his rataplan – we can't get rid of him, it seems, and on he goes, it's rim-shots now, and brushes too, he is the most ingenious sort. The crowds then come and go, they have a pattern, probably innate, like starlings do, and on and on Melinda sings.

*

Melinda's asking me, 'Should I have another face tattooed on my face,' and I'm saying that snakes on the forearms are the best thing, and here is Goran, running up, 'Come on, into our building,' and he pulls us up some green stone steps, leaps of five at a time.

The drummer tags along, we hope to lose him, but those drummers – we all have one, keeps you marching on ... Melinda says,

'This isn't our building, Goran – see, it's full of other people's people,' and Goran scoffs,

'Everyone does it – you put your guys in, where they see the empty offices – no one in these clerks' pentagons knows who is who and who's stepped out, and who is ordering who, what's on that floor and what is anyone called – you just move in. It's ours. In part and name.'

We wander round. Melinda says, 'If we are a bloc, we three, I want some islands – for weekends ... And silver sand.'

I say, 'We have no hope. Our arbitrary places, junked and tacked together – makes no sense.'

Melinda says to me, 'Your people's mostly poor, so things for you are easy – they're too busy being poor to make a fuss. My lot, though – it's culture. Reading novels, looking at brocades – it tries my eyes,' and indeed, she blinks.

Goran is angry, 'Of course it's all been done before,' he shouts, 'and failed. Depends of course what failure means. "Before" – that is a hard one too – we have a time that rushes on one way, you can't go back, or even look there – it's always new, although it smells of old. We are an alliance of the good guys – that should be enough, for sure! The economics will line up in fours when we have set this up – some smuggling, copying things, and find some actors who'll strip off, maybe some armies for the movie scenes ... You have to think new ways, new things.'

I think, but do not say, 'It doesn't sound like new,' and Goran shouts,

'Now, you stupid bastards – now is our chance, before they find tall poppies to replace the swept-aways. See how my guys are loyal! They're waiting for their pay,' and so they are, they wave their guns, those in security, and there go guys like us who're climbing on the catwalks, waiting for another storm to sweep us three away, and leave some space for them.

'See!' shouts Goran, pulling someone from a room, a closet.

'She's young,' says Melinda, coolly.

'I know that,' says Goran: 'She doesn't.'

Tattooed on her forearms there are two plump snakes, in red and green. The forearms – they too are plump and beautiful, the best I've ever seen – 'Think,' Goran says, 'Niobe here, she's some executive, across a table from you, and she lays them out – those arms, those snakes. What strength! Profundity. It makes you think.'

'The snakes are each different,' Niobe says, and I say,

'Yes, we've seen that.'

She has piercings, her face is embossed with them. Melinda says,

'I could get another body tattooed on my body,' Goran ignores her – 'Forget the piercings, those are out of time. It's all the rest ...' he says. He points to me and says to her, 'This guy's a fetishist. Gets buried in a box.'

'I quite like fetishists,' Niobe says.

'Quite? Quite like?' shouts Goran. 'Fuck you – this guy's a hero, almost. Myself – I have no fear.' He looks around: 'I've learned fear's not worthwhile, not the time, the stress. But this guy – a terrible experience, big pearls of fear all over – and never learnt a thing! Now, he's even more afraid. All that experience for nothing. For still more fear.'

He's right.

And Niobe is the grandest thing we've ever seen. Fished out at random. What a catch – for Goran.

'This goddam doorman's suit,' he says, pulling at it. 'I wear it only so I see who's bringing people in and out. And to be near the door, if there's events, attacks...'

I ask, 'Your people here – what are they busy with?'

'How should I know?' he asks. 'Nothing, I expect. The thing is loyalty, answering to me.'

Melinda says, 'We should all leave, go to our places,' and I say in mine they wouldn't know me, I'm just contracted, and she says, 'Well, that's fine, you are the sailor, husband forgotten, crawling up the beach to take your throne,' and Goran says, 'Nah – his place doesn't have a sea, just rivers, often dry,' then he explains,

'We did it all at school. It seems that Marx got tired of all the treachery, people not rising up, all that. And so – there's transmigration – Nietzsche took the business over. His stuff locked in a cabinet, they didn't let us read.'

I say, 'Transmigration – you mean old Karl's soul flew off and into ...'

'Not souls, you fool,' says Goran. 'You can't believe in them. Fear – that's the thing. It makes the history. You know the world is falling down, and with some luck you'll die before it happens to you, and never mind the rest of us. So – what's the point, in fear?'

Melinda says, 'Those snakes – maybe they're full of sacred wisdom, but they're quite upside down – they point down to her hands. They should climb up – this way they're sneaking out.'

Niobe says, 'Yes, the guy had got the picture downside up,' and Goran says,

'Yes, that's the best way. Too much reading – quizzing the pictures – screws up your brain. Things as they are: – that is the trick. Things as they fall out. Don't go back and twist them round. Melinda – if you go back where you came from – will you change a thing? And you,' he points at me. 'You'll never save a life or carry out an execution. Stay with the guy who sees it clear. With me.'

The drummer, though he's never stopped a soft shoofar shoofar, just idling on, his skin against the lazy skins – now perks up, bangs out a volley, brings some plaster down.

'Even if they give me thirty years,' says Goran. 'Niobe's still ripe and waiting.'

'Who'll be there in thirty years, to keep you in the jail?' Melinda asks: 'It's clear, the cash is finished – we are going down. Remember all the signs of ending – Russians trying things another way, the Germans going mad, a mortal finish, long announced. Curtain – then applause or boos. The French – throwing Algerians in the Seine, even now it makes me sad.'

'It's true,' says Niobe. 'You need a lot of soldiers, and it bankrupts you. Nothing to be done. You have to pay them, they've got all the guns ...' and Goran says,

'I'm sure my people came in off the steppes. There! – that was space, quite infinite, and time as well: riding the horses up and down, burying princesses and their jewellery. But now, you see it's spread to us – the massacres. One time, things broke down in a place, they started up again elsewhere ... but now, there's nowhere left. And what comes next?'

He looks around, excited, and he shouts,

'It's cannibalism! Back to our roots and capture guys and swallow them!'

Melinda says, 'It's like the poem says, "They walk and walk, in the night." How true.'

'If it all must disappear,' says Goran. 'I have it in my mind – to leave, at least – a wall.'

'Those have bad names,' says Melinda.

'Not upstanding,' Goran says. 'One lying down, that's done its work, or maybe not yet found a boundary.'

For and against those that may come next.

He says, 'Melinda, your people will do the curlicues. Mine – we're experts in alphabets – we shall do the message. Yours,' he points to me, 'Can carry slabs.'

I say, 'That won't leave them happy.'

Melinda says, 'Happy? Who's unhappy, carting blocks?'

'What shall I do?' Niobe asks – 'Mine looks the shortest stay on earth –' Melinda cuddles her and says, 'That's even longer for you up in paradise.' It doesn't reckon, and Goran says to her, 'You can correct the spelling,' and on the wall.'

The drummer asks, 'My job?'

'That's easy,' Goran says, 'Yours is "keep the beat". The sun will crack our skulls and dull our hands and suck the shade – you just keep an even beat until you see the time has come – then faster, faster, till it ends. The final rataplan.'

'Spelling's the most important part,' Niobe says.

'No one said it wasn't,' I say. 'That's why you go to school.'

Melinda says, 'Almost any message will do, since it isn't known who'll read it.'

'That's not the case with me,' the drummer says: 'Music isn't random, though no one at all may be listening to it.'

Goran says, 'Gently now – stick to our parts, and history can't shuffle them around. If no one reads the stuff, it's all the same, we'll never know.'

'The other guys out there will peer,' Melinda says, 'And think we're doing something secret they can steal,' and Goran says it's the one thing that isn't worth their while, and sure, it can keep us busy till the end, material production too – it may not be Persepolis, but doing it this way, it can't fall down, it doesn't need to last, the guys will be in work, they'll get some cash ...

'Really,' says Niobe, 'I could cry. The strangeness of it all.'

'Really!' Goran says. 'It's always strange. Maybe, if the drummer guy could find another instrument, something more nuanced, lyrical, it would give your tears a different course. More heartbreak, too.' He asks the drummer, 'Could you do a cimbalon? That'd be a compromise, if you couldn't play the harp.'

'She just needs bringing out, Niobe does,' Melinda says. 'We really aren't quite strange – we are a team, it's just our countries are so disparate – that's where the strangeness lies. It seems they don't belong. As for our end – well, it all ends, you know,' and Goran points at me and says,

'This guy, you think he is an idiot, his country – he doesn't even live in it, but he's got a policy on dolphins, his guys haven't got a sea,' and I am irritated, and I say,

'I can do policies on lots of other things,' and Niobe puts her lovely arms, her wise, foresightful snakes, around my neck, and says, 'You're not an idiot, you just need someone warm and true to curl around you, tell you that the day is beautiful and not to fear the night,' and Goran says,

'Yes, that's the spirit, and it's true, for sure,' but there creeps in some jealousy. Melinda says her country runs itself, but mine's just ants in panic, just waiting till they find a general to shoot some guys and burn their huts, and make them settle down, and 'why is that?' she asks – and Niobe says she can't wait for the answer, but there's one, for sure, and so we swing along together, friends once more.

Goran says, 'The message on the wall? Long? Short? Who cares? Anything that links with something else – that, we call a system. Old Bukhara – did I come from there? The ancestors that made me? Yes! – the apricots – the day before the blossom, all foretold ...Well, you could make the message "We were built to last." You read that as you like – it's not how long the message is, it's how big are the characters it's written in.'

'Goran is losing it – the window, the opportunity, the interim, the chance to make the difference, to transform,' Melinda says: 'We must prepare to run, and everything will stay the same, always renewing. All always identical. New bosses. It should console. Does it?' She turns to me. 'Your box, where you were buried – it seems quite meaningless, inconsequential. Doesn't mean a thing to me. I guess it does to you.'

'No, no,' I say. 'It seems to have no meaning, just its consequence – which has no meaning either. Just anxiety,' and she says that maybe they didn't dig a hole, the box was in a space, laid out, with marble all around, and even flunkeys, like a catafalque, with candles at the corners, black, and mistresses, gangsters too, all filing past – the tributes, haikus even – no drummer that's for sure, you'd have heard him, his drums at least.... Just my straw poked through the lid for air, my breath that rasps inexorable, a monster's threefold lungs, and sucking, sucking till the dome above implodes – and I am free! See! – the cuirassiers like gold and silver beetles on their backs, some explosion, that! – see their arms and legs, waving, still synchronised, the mourners thrown in heaps like chips of anthracite.

It all explodes! I'm free!

I say, 'Melinda, tell me about the States, and 42nd Street – you must remember it, like it was redemption,' and she says,

'Inside, my life is terrible. Your box was nothing. Those Americans – they've always been at war, and no one seems to notice. Good or bad, it just goes on – even on the street, they talk and talk. On and on, it goes – inconsequential. You tie the big guys' hands, they go on kicking with their feet. This interim, hiatus, leaderless – it doesn't mean a thing. Order and anarchy – the same guys do them both. Now, don't object, I've answers ready if you do.'

I'm sure she does. Besides, I don't object. She says, 'Niobe knows it all. I'll educate her.'

'She knows nothing,' I say.

'Just think,' she says, 'The Street – those porno cinemas – all done by actors! What a fraud, a perversion. Did you know?'

'Everybody knows,' I say. 'Maybe it's like the wars – a fraud that people like.'

She considers this. Maybe it doesn't make sense, even to her. She says,

'We'll be cast out, and Goran first of all. But then – a wall like that, you only need a tiny space, two guys can do it all, if that's the way it has to be.'

I say to Niobe, 'I confess – my country's full of things that I don't understand. The families, clans, tribes, religions. Cattle. Often I am frightened – not like here, you're scared of cops, the world, all that ... back there, I'm scared of no police, no ends of things. What scares me are the uniforms with the bogeymen inside, the corpses of guys who're not what we'd call dead.'

She says, 'Perhaps you should be the sailor, always afraid, so never getting off his ship, not seeking the way home, stuck with his crew of vestal sirens. I thought the sailor might be Goran – but it's you ... I'm not afraid. I took the first step, being free and then the second, putting on my snakes.'

'I don't think that living here's at all the same,' I say. 'As living back in Africa, in what's quite a different way. The warriors. The anxiety.'

‘Some guys in your place,’ she says, ‘they’re worried about dolphins. That’s surely fun.’ She’s a fine person, and I fear for her as well.

‘Go, go go!’ shouts Goran, legs slashing down like shears, down the front steps, in strides of seven, even more: ‘We’re finished here ...’ and out we go.

‘My people! They’re not proud of me. Not happy,’ Goran says. ‘New guys have come, they’re in, we’re out. Our project’s stalled, officially. Our union of the good guys – that’s all done, alas.’

It never seemed a good idea,’ Melinda says.

*

The drummer’s drum has tripped him, the beat goes skewed, he rolls and hurts – dud catherine wheel, curled around his drum hugged close. A ‘phut!’. Now, he’s ripped apart, he and his instrument destroyed, and Goran says,

‘Well, that’s a blessing! Off with Mister Sticks. No more the tippytap, the wristy time tocked out. Wow – what a bore!’

Here we are, without a project: nor a ministry to boss. Mister Stick's tick-tock has stopped, and us – we're between the movements…

'Sex with Goran,' says Niobe, 'Is like eating butterflies. He's so delicate, hesitant.'

I say, 'Maybe he thinks you'll tell on him. Your age. The cops.' She goes on,

'Melinda – she's like an Arab grande dame, naive and earthy.'

'She's not Arab. She was planted among them, and didn't root,' I say.

'Well, so you know it all,' she says, 'And yet you're still afraid.'

'If you saw those Dinkas – the country where I was – the warriors. They're big alarming guys. Really big, like buildings,' though it's much more than just from them, the fear.

Goran and I don't want to go back, back where we've just come from. Most places are like that. 'Women are different,' Goran says. 'They don't have countries,' and so the subject's left.

'Well, Niobe,' Melinda says. 'Let's start with you – what is it that you want: to be good, or do good? Do bad, or be it?'

‘That running down the stairs,’ Niobe says. ‘My shoes! The good thing is take them off. What I want to be? To know something no other person knows.’

‘I’m speechless,’ says Melinda. ‘That doesn’t fit at all, nor even sounds like muddling through. It doesn’t suit your forceful things – those snakes, they must belong to something you have planned, laid out.’

‘Nonsense, she has no plan – and this guy too, it’s all made up, there’s no Dinkas on his territory,’ Goran says, and laughs at me. ‘And Mister Sticks plays on, even if you can’t hear him. And on, and on. And we must dance to him.’

‘What’s your story, Niobe?’ I ask.

‘Mostly I seem to follow people,’ she says, and I see her teeth are pointed like a raptor’s, and it makes her more like humankind – ‘And we go from place to place, without a reason, often under just the sky, the sky, and they call for me to do something, to perform. But,’ and she smiles round at us, ‘I can’t dance. Or only like everyone can.’

‘That’s a bit like almost nothing,’ Melinda says, disappointed.

‘We three didn’t manage much,’ says Goran, ‘But at least Niobe hasn’t had to carry weapons, not like us.’

Then Niobe reaches up and kisses Melinda: ‘But – I can spin,’ she says.

And she can. Silently she spins and spins. You expect something discrete and elastic with the feet, but with her, it all comes from the head – her hair shoots out like rays, like yellow straw on a hut's roof, the thatch.

'You wish there was Mister Sticks, just to show that there is time, and that in the end it passes and it stops,' Goran whispers, 'Even Blue Grass music would grab better here ...'

He's seen it all before. Melinda says,

'What do you think of, Niobe, while you spin?' but the spinning, silent, goes on, and at last Niobe, still turning slowly, answers,

'You're not supposed to think. Sometimes something comes to you, but it isn't what you want.'

'Well, I guess that's dangerous living,' Goran says, as she winds down and starts to teeter to a stop. She throws her head back – those teeth! She shouts, she roars, you can see right down inside her, not sexy, you can almost see down to the fire, and she shouts, 'Where do I come from...?' and Goran recognises the line, the song, and starts to hum along until she's quiet and they're both still.

It's most impressive, quite inconclusive. Melinda must have heard this, some such, long ago, live or from the record stores on 42nd Street.

'O fuck,' I think. 'Is this what's left, of all the plans? Flight and re-build…'

*

'I love Niobe,' says Melinda. 'It's a real passion. I can't think where it comes from. She could be a daughter, sister. Not a friend. Love, passion, is unequal exchange, of course, or no exchange at all. It's good to hold it all inside myself, and feel good, and anxious. But I don't know what the passion's for, and where she comes into it. That Goran, now, he wanted something erotic. With me! What d'you think of that?'

I say, indifferent, 'You must have been devastated.'

'In your box, what did you think of?' she asks.

'You have to make some space and light,' I say, 'It's no good thinking about mottoes on some wall. No good thinking of three countries – one with capital, one with the fixers, and one with guys that do the work. That was Goran's plan. It might have worked like that – your country's full of rich guys, Melinda, Goran's territory's full of wise guys, mine has lots of hands and feet. But – maybe it's not like that at all. My guys use their hands and feet to stand around, Goran's are smugglers, yours go to the theatre while they've got the cash. And when the cash runs out, they stop.'

'The idea's good,' Melinda says. 'Instead of how it works in every place, rich, fixers, and the guys who make it work – you have three countries, each one specialised, and bonded close. It would be tough on some ....' I say,

'It's up to guys who do the work to think of dignity, of turning things around. But – it's not like that at all,...' and on I go till Melinda says,

'Your box? How'd you trick it out?'

'You need a tree, with flowers and fruit. Some steps, and water. And someone else – yes, but not so close they breathe your air. And rain – and music too. But all without excess, you mustn't fantasise – at times you talk, you shout and scream, you sweep the leaves. There is no sun or moon, of course, but dark and day.'

'That's quite remarkable. We never could have known all that,' she says.

When I was in the box, all I could do was breathe. The calm, the architecture, all comes after, long after. I do not tell her that, but, perhaps, she knows.

'Rooks,' I say, 'You need them, they give a sense of space, of doing things together that doesn't put a weight on you. Rooks ...'

Melinda says, 'Yes, magnificent. Without rooks, where would you be – there they are, high in their castles, their masts, dipping in the wind and clinging on. Singing like cracked sailors, the land, the land! And the gossip of landfall. Yes, Niobe and rooks – that's me.'

Me too, I see.

'Niobe could be a dancer,' Melinda says.

'She's a dancer now, already,' I say. 'What you want, Melinda, is Coppelia. An automaton. That is wicked! You should stick to what we do – sending troops to here and there. Goran too – though his guys mostly do their things by instinct. We're the real people, Melinda, with our views – those leaders are our shadows. When they're swept away, we're here, untouched. Us – philosophers. We never fail – only executives do that. Do you prefer the better, or the good? One or the other, that's our trade. You must remember, and live up to that.'

'She can't sing, so she could be a chanteuse – make a disc, and disappear,' Melinda says.

'Don't dare, Melinda,' I tell her: 'Love and desire and doing Goran down – that's not your trade, you risk disaster there.' She says,

'Those little countries – big ones like yours as well, that's big because they're full of poor that scarcely grow that stuff you couldn't eat ...' and she makes a face, 'Like porridge that you grind between your thighs; or softened with your spit, it tastes of thistle – what's the use of those peoples, countries even if they're big? Voting for thieves, my dear, that's their ideal.'

I say, 'Melinda, you must think in terms of centuries,' and in she jumps,

'Yes, centuries! Goran's guys, they think like that, that's why he stares around and screws the young, the new, he finds them in the closet, seduces them in elevators – going down or going up, try anything to leave the past, those landscapes where the tanks have shed their tracks, like snakeskins ...' and she's back. To Niobe.

'I'll find a way,' Melinda says: 'I'll stop that Goran. I shan't put him in a box and dig him up. Who knows what you had done,' she asks me, and I don't respond, 'But surely you deserved at least a decent tumulation ... Goran has destroyed our innocence, somehow we must try to punish him, and get it back.'

My answer would be feeble, so I'm silent.

'Oh,' says Melinda. 'Of course I won't bomb them. I just want to deal with Goran, no one thinks to save a guy like that. Articles, short movies – planted well. A bank that doesn't lend. Rights? That always works a bit – and criminals. They must have lots where he is based, and then there's shady guys that live with us ... His country – they will get the hint, and dolphins won't come into it. In the end they'll give us what I want, and if they don't, well, no one's clean and innocent, just push a little. Then, there's guys with guns, freelance, the last resort but one – and in the end they'll yield, and all will turn out true, just like we said, and if they don't,' and she smiles at me. 'Then there's hotter, harder stuff, and on we go ...' and she is smiling generally, and probably her friends do too.... If Goran goes no one will know, it's good we are the good guys, his, over there, are pretty bad and unpredictable, and if a big cheese goes down, well, who will care, another comes, and on we go.

I feel like – doing treachery: I tell Goran – 'Melinda's after you. To save Niobe, for herself.'

'That sounds equivocal,' he says. 'Perhaps we should walk to India, Niobe – get away from everything, not take a map.'

'That's not me,' Niobe says. 'Though Isfahan appeals. If there's a God, they built it right to suit Him: spot on.'

'I've got caught up, it seems,' says Goran. 'In some new world order. Me and my guys – we're in the slot. It's not to do with you, Niobe, that's for sure.'

'I didn't think it was,' Niobe says, 'Melinda – she's too masculine: Those droopy songs, her drummer pal. No, I'm the Mediterranean type, early to sprout, then overblown for years and years.'

'For certain it's the food,' says Goran, 'Lambs' brains with capers – fun, but too precocious.'

I say, 'This order, Goran, it is peace with soldiers, you know that. You have to stand in threes, and if you form a four, or in your case a two – they're after you. It's not to do with suffering, that's quite incidental, these campaigns go on until the cash is spent. And then they add the horrors up.'

Goran says that's quite too trite, because down there, my country, there's a storm that never ends, and I say, 'Goran, fuck you, take your *Braut* and leave,' and he laughs and asks 'Where's brotherhood?'

'We don't ask you what you want,' I tell Niobe. 'Because we think we've sacrificed you.' 'You sacrifice people all the time,' she says.

'Yes, but randomly. If you must walk to India – let's see you take some warriors with spears, some Dinkas – I can ask a friend ...' I say.

'I've all I need, my skin,' she says. 'No spears and bodyguards. Melinda, she's all right, I guess, but all that sex, the drumming,' and Goran says, 'It's sex that makes the history. The beat.'

'I guess for you guys, that's all good enough,' Niobe says. 'The drummer in your heads, as on you go. Tap tap. The new world order – it's a hash of planks when you are going under. While you sink, you shout 'Niobe – we're protecting you,' and hope it buoys you up.'

I say, 'That would be something, Niobe. In time, you'll find the cries of shipwrecked sailors beautiful, and when you stand beside the sea, you'll hear the seagulls take it up – 'we loved you, Niobe, in our small way,' and we'll come into your mind.'

'I've quite enough with Goran,' Niobe says, but though she's acid, maybe she bears with him. The new world order too.

'You'll enjoy Niobe,' I tell Goran. 'She'll be the new woman.'

'What she has, I enjoy,' he says, irritably, 'And she'll be new women as often as it suits. It's being hunted I can't take.' I say,

'It's terrible, Goran – I must admit my share, and I'm contrite. I'm born a traitor – I confess. But between you and your country – we can't differentiate. The two are indissoluble. Down goes the one, the other too, perforce. That is Melinda's law.'

*

He says, 'It's not my country, as you know. I've a contract. Doesn't cover Niobe, and if my guys break it, what am I to do?'

'We all have contracts,' I say. 'What does yours say? Mine says to follow sounds of cash – that isn't much, and doesn't bind, there are no other offers. They – we – tried socialism, didn't much enjoy, and now it's capital. That's paint, clotted in the can. Promise eternal, like a stone.'

'I don't know what my contract promises – why bother, when you can't enforce?' Goran asks.

*

'Niobe's too young. And too desirable,' Melinda says.

'Nonsense,' I say. 'No one's too young, and no one's that desirable. Besides, Melinda, your country has a past and so must you. All pasts are painted over with forgetting paint, and that is right, they weren't loved while they were going on – and now, you lift a corner of the canvas – there's the dead flesh.'

She's irritated – maybe she thinks of guys her country shovelled in the river. Those guys, they're all forgotten, but the country, what it did, you can't forget. There – it's on the maps, the flags, the stamps and logos.

She turns on me, 'Hey! Your country, do you call it fractured or bisected? Nicely split in two, and angry guys – the ones that maybe tried to ransom you? That will go on, no doubt you did something unforgivable, and that won't disappear – I see the shrivelled skulls like walnut shells, hanging on your belt.'

I say, 'So what – the belt is mine. It helps me cover up,' and then she says that Goran's country can't exist, it just split off, rebels, gangs, bands, all that.

'That's in our heads,' I say. 'What is and ought to be. It doesn't count, your country being how you'd like it. Where are we going, where do you want to take us, Melinda? To save Niobe from Goran, and the things he did, he may have done? Or else – it's his country that you're after. Liberation, necessity? Our words, Melinda.'

'Try to save your people,' she says.

I say, 'Down there, the bosses – they're inscrutable. They have their rules, their contacts. Your guys, Melinda, they are part of you, they'll even take their clothes off in your room. Mine have a uniform, they wear it underneath their suits.'

Months later ...

Niobe says, 'Well! Lots of happy people, too much sand. We didn't walk, we took the bus,' and Goran says, 'Lots of sad people – I don't think we got to India. We doubled back, but left our mark. We didn't see a decent wall, though there were lots of alphabets. Perhaps another day of march ... The guys want order, and they love the new. It's putting those two words together, that's what's tough,' and then Melinda says,

'Goran, your past – it ties you down. Niobe's future – that was over there for her, within her grasp,' and they both stare at her, and wonder what she plots.

Niobe tells me, 'Burnt palaces and buried walls, that's what we didn't see, but there they were, and Goran in love pursuing me, though he was always out in front. Love. Passion, turns into drama, then ritual, and no, I'm not a believer, it doesn't seem to matter if you aren't. We travelled with some Russians, they were dirty, but precise about their clothes.'

'An adventure,' I say.

'Quite too much,' she says. 'And Goran thinking how your guys, your clans, will go to war.'

'Mine always are,' I say. 'Conflicted. It's his he needs to watch. They made a nation, all complicit, all joined up, resentful. You've been in a bees' nest too, Niobe, the politics, Goran spraypainting crossbones on the houses.'

She says, 'We wondered if we ought to feel responsible, what for, how much. And who's to blame – it can't be all Melinda,' and I say,

'You better pin all that you can on her – it's quite the human touch.'

The storm, the storm! – it swept them all away, and here they are again, the bosses. Quite similar.

Pointless, this populism, saying next time will not be the same: the wars, anabasis – then back they come. Though, of course, we have moved on – we have no choice.

Melinda sings her songs, and Goran, the liberator, is quite precarious. Melinda hums to him: '*Un vent de fronde s'est levé ce matin*', the scheming wind that lays the plots, for, after all, it is our job to plot, bring to justice, or at least to court.

Niobe is bored with both of them, Melinda and Goran.

My farmers and the cattle guys will fight until the hunger reaches them, and then they'll maybe put me in the box again and try to ransom me.

'I'm worth a war,' says Niobe, 'Though that's not what I want. But still, if history calls...'

Goran tells Melinda, 'If you want Niobe, you can have her. But you'll have to fight us first. I've gotten quite a name for liberating, and my new guys – they prize my skills ... we took the bus, and nearly came to India.'

'I don't think much of any of you,' says Niobe. 'But I mean no harm.'

*

I tell the doctor, 'Something is happening to my feet.'

He says, 'Maybe you want a cruise. Perhaps you work with fish. Your colleague, Mister Kite – he has dreams too, but not of fish. His case is flight. I can tell you this – it's all in both your minds, so there's no fear for privacy. He drops acid, I declare. He's suspended, he can't soar – it troubles him no end. It's fantasy, my friend, you're looking for a home, the lot of you, and some go walking back, some take the bus, while you,' he means me, 'you have made a perilous choice, exploring caves, the sea, the sea – shipwreck, transmogrifying witches – there's no wonder someone's spell has grappled on your mind. You must believe that somewhere there is peace, a pregnant wife, some kids that look like her, a dog incontinent, those slaves you beat, the epicenes that giggle at the bedroom door – one day you'll scramble up the beach, a merman, and waiting there they'll be ...'

'No, no,' I shout, 'Forget all that, the wife, the palace, figments – it's my feet, that swish....'

'The trouble is,' the doctor says, 'you're always moving round. Your countries change their boundaries, they fight and squall, and nature doesn't help. Your job, you experts – yours is quite some game' and he sits back, proud: 'Musical palaces. That's its name.'

There's nothing to be done. Another malady adheres, incurable as ever.

'You guys,' Niobe says. You're all in black and white. You too –' she points at me, '– in your box, the flowers are black, the steps are grey, the god is white, up in the shrine, so white it's quite invisible ... I need to make an impact, if I don't, I can't tell I exist. Must be in colour – honey and old rose.'

'You started well with Goran,' I say. 'Not everyone has made an expedition, never fired a shot, and come back home.'

'Yes, yes,' she says. 'But now that's done and over, that's the past! It must start over, being something new.'

'Yes, yes,' I say. 'It will, that's what it does. The first advice – only take your clothes off with your friends – don't be a singer, you must do it all the time, there's thousands watching, off comes your blood and bones and meat. Don't sing, don't be Melinda – on the street she strives for second best. You should do nothing, if you can't come out on top.' She says,

'She had a drummer,' and I say those drummers, we all have one, they're like radiation, in the end the clatter hollows out your bones, the bang, the rhythm – and she talks of nargilehs and donkeys, people in white clothes who have a coloured cushion tacked to their behind so's not to dirty when they sit, and then she says,

'Unless you live for ever, there is just no point,' and that is true, already she is grander than the rest. I say,

'Goran was a warrior – when you talk of nations, there's no way you can decide a right side or a wrong, it's loyalties and noble deaths. He had his mission. Now maybe he'll go on trial,' and Niobe says, 'Yes, that's Melinda's plan. She has a noble, righteous soul.'

*

'So far, nothing's seemed mysterious,' Niobe says.

I see her on her oracle's throne, quite stoned, the smoke, the sulphur, snakes dripping from her crown: 'That's why you're supposed to make the riddles up and tell them to me,' I say.

'Right!' she says, 'Goran now – is it true what he did? The crimes?'

'He's told you,' I say. 'Thirty years worth. You must remember. Anyway, there were lots of them together, patriots, recruits. Just think – his was the winning side ... Not Macedonia, no, not there at all! He lies, he doesn't come from there! Melinda put the pressure on, to have him lie. Her people always do. My guys, instead – no one blames them for the things they do, they have no cause, illusion, there is no history before. Nature and interests, that's all. No blame, so no responsibility, for them or me.'

'You're outside it, anyway,' she says, quite kindly. You make it up, all of it …'

'I don't think I can stand it,' I say, without thinking: 'Reality. Unreality.'

'Yes, of course you can,' she says, 'Nothing's up to you.'

She spins slowly, wistfully. Her arms, her snakes, she raises them to cover her face. As she rotates, she's all snake.

She stops, and says, 'On the expedition, they made me cover up. They didn't know about the dinosaurs, if they were real. Dinosaurs or snakes – to them it was the same. They didn't know my snakes are teachers, keys. In their heads, all was quite cosy, things abstract didn't seem to bother them.' She stares dreamily, then asks me,

'Did dinosaurs have rights? Or is it just us that gives and takes them, never telling animals what they've got, or maybe don't? And if we are not there?'

I say, 'Dinosaurs don't give each other rights. We can't have expectations either.'

'Well, you know about these things,' Niobe says. 'If I believe you or I don't, I'm not sure we get on further.'

I want to ask – further on to what?

Melinda says, 'Love. That is all that's left. We've reached the last resort, love comes and goes, you can't do much about it – it's the storm. Like 'flu. But not a sentimental thing, that love, but grim and with vendettas.'

'I don't want it then,' Niobe says, 'It's worse than Goran.'

'Every dolphin's called Vassili,' I tell Niobe.

'I knew you knew just about everything,' she says. 'Goran says that when they got their uniforms, they stood in line and giggled. Their names – they mostly didn't fit – father was this, and mother that – forbidden fruit, I guess – then off to shoot and loot.'

'It's all quite trite,' I say. 'We should all have the same names, like at the start. In the fruit garden.'

'Did anyone look out for the swept-aways?' Niobe asks.

'I don't expect so,' Melinda says. 'There's replacements, ambition to go with. And the fear of heavy things that fall and pin you down.'

'If Goran's a criminal,' Niobe asks, 'who is not?' I say:

'Maybe everyone should have a trial. Not you, Niobe – when Goran plucked you from the closet, you were innocent as a moth, I'm sure.'

'I like you,' Niobe tells me. 'Because you don't want to improve anything, it's just to do your crap job well, like knowing the names of all those fish, and being scared of your guys and not wanting to do them good.'

'Did Goran want to improve?' I ask myself. 'Those sacrifices ...'

'You have to welcome the future,' Niobe says. 'I hope to make my living there.'

'Melinda had a fearsome past,' I say. 'Humans the ones involved. Relatives – I guess being related makes it worse – you're twinned with badness from the start. Now, she's prim.'

'Yes, being upright makes it worse,' Niobe says –

'The what she does,' I finish for her.

'Sex has been quite discomforting,' Niobe says.

'You're lucky – it can be worse things than that. But why tell me? I can't feel for you,' I say.

'Melinda and Goran – maybe I'm part of their plan for betterment,' she says. 'It makes me retch.'

'They both go marching on,' I say, 'while I'm just stuck. I know how it will end, my coming, my return. Since in that box I didn't die, there's not much alternative. Up the beach, coming to confusion, turning my back on the boundless threatening sea – those awful human creatures in the caves, the magic – o no! what's waiting for me in the grass, under the palm trees, through the lion gate ...'

'There's good ways of killing people, but you need to know the law,' I say.

'Goran's been freed, at any rate,' Niobe says. 'Melinda's on a course – this time, it's cajun fiddle.'

I say, 'They like their guys to broaden out. Profs at the conservatoire, that is....'

'I often see Melinda,' says Niobe, as though that means a lot.

'Look, Niobe,' I say. 'We could see my Africa in the movies – that's the only way.'

She's reluctant: 'Don't go touching me, in the cinema.'

'Naturally. It isn't that,' I say.

She says, 'Where we two went, it wasn't Africa. It was squalid, or we were, but we were on the move.'

We watch the movie. People dance, complain to camera, live in dull big family groups. Some wear too many clothes, and some wear none.

'What do you think, Niobe? You've an idea of my work?' I whisper, ask.

'Ah, the movies,' she says not listening. 'I feel I could go up there, on the stage, and mediate or arm. The sides – they are so clear, the power of flesh – like mine – so great. It's all in gelatine, like boiled goose or duck. I stick my fork in, and resolve it, the impasse.'

'Is that all?' I ask, disappointed. 'Your response?'

'It's all striving,' I go on, whispering. 'In Africa. Those lives – in the movie, striving doesn't show. On screen, they're all stuffed birds. In life, their life, every moment is decisive. My job's just measuring, it doesn't impact a bit.'

Niobe's not so sure, but she is wrong. 'Goran's war,' I say. 'It was lambs slaughtering each other, with proud cries. It softened him, though he's still responsible, of course. Not that he's being held to account.'

She says, 'He was very anxious about bus timetables. Something of the past came off on him.'

I go on, 'You should have seen Melinda, long ago. Bum-strutting on the table – some culture congress. Not singing, but wow! her scene. Short leather skirt and all.'

'No!' says Niobe. 'Not like Tina Turner?'

'More,' I say. 'Even sweatier. Always part gay carnival queen, part moping prince designing scaffolds. When she's up there, Niobe – look at the lights, look at the colours, how many there are, blue, rose and buttercup.'

We imagine it all, Melinda's show.

I say, 'Niobe, you could be more than that, I believe in you.' I can't imagine what I'm saying, but this is the moment.

'I'm nothing,' Niobe says.

'I believe in nothing,' I say, and we laugh.

'You guys,' she says. 'You pass over everything, as if you're innocents, and hollow, like drums played by who knows who ... I don't trust you, not a bit.'

The new order

'China's splitting up, I see,' says Goran. 'Was it you?' he asks Melinda, and we all laugh, Melinda modestly.

'When we walked to India, or nearly so,' he goes on, 'we didn't think it was a way to start an empire, did we, dear?' and he chucks Niobe under her lovely chin. She pulls away, and says,

'The Americans? What's become? We don't hear too much of them. Their food! What treats! Maybe the secret's lost ...'

Melinda says, 'They split up too. Those big bluff places – they got so disorderly, it's best they're cut down to righteous size.'

Goran says, 'Well, to abandon hope's fascistic. We should follow science – those guys did, or thought they did – it's just the science was all bad! Apocalypse! That "fry or starve"! Just a newsman's trick. And all the buying guns and stuff – you knew where that would lead,' and we all nod, the evidence is there, 'abundant', says Niobe, and she turns to me and says it's sad my guys still have big lands and nothing much to do, except what they had always done, though now they know they're poor, not even warriors – and: 'It's not your fault,' she tells me, and I say,

'I never thought it was. It may be irksome, but they say some will be poor and fight, and some are rich and do the same, and who am I to intervene in nature's law? It's striving, striving, Niobe, that is all it is.'

She whispers to me, 'We share so many things. The names of fish – or eels, perhaps. As for your feet – I love neurotics,' and I say,

'No, no, I'm cured. No fishy tales about me, Mister Kite is in rehab, there's no neuroses now. The world has turned out plastic, and I've lost my fear, things as they are have changed – Melinda's finger does its work, and we adjust. Besides, Niobe, I can't cleave to you, I've a woman from way back, haven't even thought of her for years ...' and she waves her snakes at me – or are they eels? – and says, 'I can't see that working out.' And nor can I, it didn't then, whatever working out can mean, and then she puts her arms, her snakes, around my neck, and there she is: her throne, the oily smoke, riddles and taradiddles, and I'm lost in great hypotheses, the future lies within her guess, and there! I'm crawling up the beach – over there the funeral mounds, the palace full of tarts and archers, that old dog – its time has past, and ...'

'No, no,' Niobe cries. 'You don't need that! Go back on board, your ship – it needs no port, it sails for ever, touring the witches' caves, its sails of finest foil, of gold, the sailors qualified, discrete. And if we want, I'm up there too – up on the prow ... protector' and on, and on, she goes.

*

Goran says, 'We might have got to India – it's all in pieces, always was. My forbear Alexander – he left little pools of Greece ...' and we all snigger – 'Walking to India as he did. Leading that horse. They couldn't even say his name – Iskandar was the closest.

Modernity is not for them, nor yet postmodern stuff. The dead – they're dropped into the river – not like China where you're buried in your Daimler. Wonder if they'll excavate them, with all that bling, like those princesses on the steppe, who thought they'd try on necklaces and crowns of finest gold for all eternity – got dug up instead, and put on show.'

Melinda interrupts. 'The trouble is,' she says, 'We know the ancestors were pretty smart. They could make rope and do accounts on clay,' and she looks round at us, and our mouths drop open, wonder and ignorance prevail, 'We're not so smart that we can keep the structure up. It all falls down!' she says.

'It's you, Melinda!' Goran says. 'You drum along, you make the world vibrate. You push, it rocks, it splits apart,' and she smiles.

I think, 'If she could sing quite perfect, we'd have order,' but then Goran says, 'Our evolution's at an end. This 'now' is as good and bad as it will ever get for us,' and then Melinda scoffs,

'You've listened to that Cal Tech guy! He thinks our heads have reached their boundary. Him! – he's small in everything, his head is not his least, his tiniest, bud. You guys want order, that is easy – our destiny lies in just the opposite; see how it multiplies, it spreads! Not striving: – challenge and confusion. Disorder – that is what we need, where we must thrive, that is our future, ever more: disorder and chaos. That is what the magic brings,' and she stares at Niobe, who does half a spin and stops, 'And science too, and all the stuff we do. If we don't love it, chaos, we are fools. The storm, the storm, that is where we come alive. Listen! the rooks, they hear it from afar, they flap their wings and sing their broken songs.

Those guys, those leaders – you gather them together in one spot – of course they're swept away, and no one cares, and no one looks! It's quite irrelevant. The storm – bigger and broader, on and on! See how the clouds swoop down, black wings, and – is it wind, or is it rain? that blows us all away and makes a desert, piles of junk, and ponds of mud, see – the writhing things, beginnings without ends, the dirty plates of finest gold that glister where they're tossed. That, my friends, is things as they are, they were, and will be as they change!'

'This old story,' Goran says. 'How many times? Women – find an income, leech on, and create confusion,' and Melinda joins in, 'Men, trudge to their banal destiny. Goran – what's up? Missing the other guys in the tent? The sleeping bags? The hugs?'

Niobe says, 'It's true, men are prose,' that could mean anything, but it's all chewed over; in the box, alone – it doesn't bother if you're man or woman. Or if China's just one bowl, or dropped and shattered – it's not the number of the shards, it's the process, shock of the floor. Goran follows what I think, and says,

'Yes, better to be in India, born as a swarm.'

'It's good not to have to face that war crimes rap,' says Goran. Melinda says,

'I dropped a word. It's what you do for friends. You little fish – you're thrown back in the pond, we hope that we don't meet you in the dark, is all.'

'I ...' Goran starts.

'No, no,' she says. 'No "I". If it's not "we" or "they", some motives and some politics, I just don't want to hear your bloody anecdotes. Think Greek, so when you've plunged your spear, then wipe it off and talk of is and ought, and why is "is", or maybe not.'

But then she ponders, and she changes register, 'That Marx – a student of the Greeks, no less! And how it could be changed, and shovel old philosophy down, in the hole, and then – confusion, turmoil, hammering the old and making particles that buzz around. Hurrah, the revolution – then a million years of growing beans and writing villanelles! The change that brings the stasis, men crowing on the pile of crap that they call history. Men crowning men, the triumph of the species, Narcissus triumphans! You fucking Greeks – we follow you, we cheer you on, hurrah! there's India ...! And then you all creep back. Homesick, you troglodytes! And that Odysseus, just the same – those sexy witches, magic, all refused – "oh nooo, I'm married", that's his cry, the cretin, renounced it all, and drift off home, some clumsy textile worker cheating him, some ancient flame of his – my, what delight! And that's supposed to be an epic? A wooden horse and scuffles in the sand? A wooden horse you push! Some carpenter's idea. At least it could have wings!'

He says, 'It's always been this way – like Niobe said, with sex it's passion, drama – and then ritual. With states – it starts with shooting, then it's jail, then harassing, and at the last – indifference. And then, sometimes, the shooting starts again. It's always been this way, like that Italian says, it all comes round, sex, politics. And if you're not liked, or difficult – look at the Indians in America ...'

'Forget that stuff,' Melinda says. 'There is no centre now, nothing to gyre around. Just take it as it comes – from now, the days will all be different.'

Now I'm going to take the brakes off,' Melinda says. 'Air brakes. When I see a place I want to go, I'll smooth a strip and land.'

'She never feels temptation,' Goran tells Niobe. 'If you feel it, sometimes you resist, and that makes up your life, the yes and no. Melinda helps you, or she does you down, she doesn't have, she doesn't give, a choice. It's quite exciting.'

I say, 'Melinda thinks of having her side win, is all.'

And there in the street she stands, no drummer and no beat, no song – just cries, a crow, a gull, a hawk, her head thrown back, a call for war and scavenging, and looking down on things, and seeing heads like match-heads far below – triumph or frustration? Hunger, that's for sure, those beaks must find some flesh to pull and tear.

Niobe cries –

'She calls, she calls! And we are ready,' and she laughs and claps her lovely hands.

Melinda says, 'Those seven Chinas – I've got some guy from Rome to tramp out there and make an inventory. I like to cut a deal with warlords – they've a word that they can keep, not like those pop-up guys who come and go. The trouble, though, with guys that say they've been and seen miraculous things, is often they've stayed in their room inventing off the screen. I bet this type brings us a pizza, spaghetti, all that stuff, and says he found it in some desert space, and how the ministers there wear hats that's made of coral, shoes of lapis lazuli. Then there's all those Americas – they specialise: one is a movie set, another is just slot machines and shuffle boards. Our information's meagre, and the roads are poor. Maybe we'll start with

China – they'll have bits of wall for sale ...' and Goran says he'd rather start a wall anew, the buildings there are made of paper scraps – they fall, and then they're back to scrolls that's lying everywhere upon the ground, though everyone is free to scrawl and decorate – and sharing beds with pigs, and doing gym before the dawn, and growing wispy beards.

The Italian tells us – 'Hi guys – so, did you know, the guys here gave the Mongols a written language, or at least an alphabet, as they went riding through – and pacifist religion too? The Buddhism, like we have in Italy? – although in history, it didn't seem to work. Since then, the sand has mounted up, the clay has gone to mud and dust,' and on he goes, you get it off your laptop, all that stuff, and needn't leave the house.

'Another fraud,' Melinda says, 'Who says he went. Didn't, and so won't be paid.'

'That old China and America,' Melinda says, 'cracked when I dropped them – often, it just takes a word. The guys one day will think – "am I a part of this? Is this a part of me? No, no – let's start another page." Births of new nations, blood and screams. You see, society is made like this – the top's composers. That's what life is all about. Then, come the witches and the gamblers.'

Niobe exalts and stamps her heels. Melinda presses on – 'Goldsmiths and pearl divers – they are next. Gravediggers and DJs – they sort things out, dispose, propose. And at the bottom – there's no prejudice in this – you choose to be down there, and "bless you all the same": it's guys who don't direct and shape. They just apply – and dig and prune and bind and pray. Those are the doctors, guys with their apricots, politicos elect, the priests ... though not the shamans – they're up there,' and she waves her hands aloft.

'You see,' she goes on. 'The Indians have it right – the whole thing works because of guys who know their place – it's just they got a factor wrong: it's not hereditary ...'

'Melinda!' Goran interrupts. 'That's crap. These systems never work. There isn't one that does – you tinker, you invert, you do philosophy. You put the DJs at the top, but guys will moan and shred the tapes. The only principle is this – the guys that work for other guys, they don't direct and shape. And yet, they're where your future lies – they blow this huge balloon of capital that no one sees and no one knows how it will end: explode or suffocate us all! That is the choice – not starve or fry – that capital that no one owns will smother you or blow you all away, you guys that think you're rich, you guys that know you're poor,' and Niobe leaps up on a chair and says,

'Hurrah! I get to choose between you both!' but then Melinda says, 'Cool your exalt, young chip, there's Goran's crimes, those weigh upon his plan!'

'No, no,' says Goran. 'Guilty or not, it's past, it can't exist, it has no weight. And I've my wall to build, posterity will judge, it always does. The improvisers cannot rule the world,' and then Melinda says, 'You heard me sing, create, and draw a crowd. And with my cajun fiddling, you'll see, that's what the people want – that's improvised, and all the rest is chance, is luck, is fantasy, invention,' but we know – this isn't all, her secret's in the friends she has, from nursery and school, no, not hereditary, but surely fixed in memories.

Niobe says, 'I strolled about outside – there was that cactus, like a bear!' She laughs. 'I'd taken all my talismanic piercings out, they sap your current, now I'm full of spines, of pricks.'

Melinda gets impatient – 'Enough of this, Niobe, back to your books.'

'We rarely use them,' Niobe says, quite weakly, and politely.

'Niobe,' shouts Melinda, 'I can snuff you.'

A pause, and then she adds, 'But I won't.'

Goran says he can't say anything. We talk of justice, and he says to me, 'Maybe they had justice in their thoughts, when they came to seize and ransom you,' and I object.

'Maybe they did – but it's not clear. I wasn't ransomed, so I wasn't worth, I didn't have a price, still less a value. And – I'm not a colonist: where there are right sides, I try to find myself on all of them,' and we speak on, what is a just man, how he, she, might secure more justice from the rest, and if she, he, can't ...

Niobe says, 'I'll gut you, Melinda,' and she makes the gesture – the cut, she starts it at the genitals, the knife drives in, and then runs up, up to the line of breasts.

*

'Your evil friends,' Melinda says to her. Niobe says,

'I've only you,' and with another gesture makes a little fort, of me, of Goran: and Melinda too.

Goran says, 'Well, this splitting up – it doesn't change that much. We write our papers, deal with things. It's Africa again. In bits. I'm sorry China didn't make it – were they on a decent road? It's history – there's capitalism first, and then ...'

'You're crazy, Goran,' shouts Melinda. 'Up in your invisible balloon you don't own! It's capitalism forever, buy and sell, you should get used to it – forever, till the pouf!'

'It isn't I can't read,' Niobe says, to calm us down: 'It's I prefer that people tell me things, so I can stare right down to their eyes, and spot the lie.' Melinda ignores her, says,

'I'll get Delphine to do America, tell us all' and I think of dolphins, and I ask,

'Who's this Delphine?'

'Delphine is like the dolphins, she's a friend of man. It's men who have no friends. The battle for survival and the struggle of the suicidal – it can end the same. It needs us – angels all – to write the book, the good book no one reads. We can't do more,' Melinda says, and Goran says, no no, for sure that book is read and memorised, they shout it from the mountain tops, recite it in the dolphin depths. It's just a book. 'Now, if it was a movie,' and we laugh, the cinema has been too dangerous a place for years.

Delphine puts her mouth up close, too close, to everyone – it's like a cat's, insistent, when it wants to bite your nose. She says, 'I'll do Americas for you, and Chinas too,' but Goran says we need a ceremony before she goes – 'Just the five of us, a dancing round the fire. It's really all for you,' he says, and points at me. 'To see if you have quality. So far, you've just been underground.'

Delphine says usually that's the end, it's clear I'm quite perverse to start off in a box – 'And end up who knows where!' shouts Goran. 'That's the point, we have this party thing, and swap our brains, our clothes, and scream, and run like fireballs down the streets of this sad town, and then we'll see behind the spires and domes – the wings that bring the storm, and sweep us all away. Or maybe leave just one, with Goran's brain inside Niobe's skin!' – and there we see his fantasy, it's running down the street, its hairy back's a blanket or a mat, a shapeless thing, a blob that wants to squeeze inside your skin.

'Delphine,' says Goran. 'If you want to party, you must be the right shape, and please your host – the host is earthy, don't be fooled, there's not just heavenly hosts ...' and he rummages over her.

'No no,' she says, 'I'm just an academic, leave me be! Academe – the greatest privilege – you say just what you want, it doesn't count, but you've protection, so you think. And I shall be your missionary – go wherever you will fund me. I'll bring back the truth, you can trust....'

He says, 'Hum ho – you find that stuff, the cultures, all gratis on the web.' He starts to design her, make her over, drastically: 'Now, the hair. It must upstanding be, like the wild thorn-tree. Bronze, with those white cherry flowers ...' and she complains, and he goes on, 'The nose – not long and probing, those red nostrils carved right through into some artery – o no: a friendly monkey pug, that's what we need! The eyes – as sharp as cactus spines, to enter deep and not let go. One brown, one green – one turned within and what you might call sightless, while the other glows by night...' and he tilts his head, then tilts hers so they match – 'The mouth! What goes in and out: not food, not lewdness – no, we mustn't think of that. It's tralalas we must associate with it.... The skin – let it be as white as camels, not this veiny drip of gorgonzola ...' and he smooths away the blur and blot. 'You must convince, Delphine – the moral charge does not fire up unless you look the part – perfection, slimmer, a cleaner look than young Niobe has ...'

'Now!' he kneads her breasts, and lays them bare. 'I think – not pyramids, that's coarse, and sharp. No, no, the idea's that of loving burial mounds, with young princesses near the top, inside but waiting for the word, the resurrection,' and he shapes them – 'Princesses. Yes. Young, yes, princesses very young. And on the peaks – en cabochon, of course, the nipples – rubies or garnets,' and he turns to me, 'Whadd'ya think?'

'Garnets,' I say, and he goes on,

'Then down here,' he slides his hand down. 'A crease, a hint, not a thicket with a doe inside that's hunkered down all palpitating – no, a valley, vale, a tuft of heather, near the reluctant well – and ah yes, the belly – thereon to swim and swim, out to the magic island, indigo, the pale blue sky, green sea ...' He's quite satisfied. He turns to me – 'I'll leave the feet to you,' he says. 'You should be quite the expert there – maybe a mermaid's tail?'

I laugh, I say, 'You're going well without a help,' and Delphine says it's sparky overall, but the exercise is macho, and he says,

'It is a bit, of course, but why else would there be some gender difference – only the angels are indifferent, and they are naked, just like you. We haven't dealt with clothes at all.' So he goes on, and then Melinda comes, and hugs Niobe close and they both kiss, and so it seems the party's off already, maybe just postponed – and Delphine is dressed in red and blue, a breast is loose, and she could be the fearless one that meets the waves, and plunges up and down with them, and guides the ship towards the deep, where dolphins watch and sing their tralalas – you think she's made of wood and gold, but she is livelier than me or you, that eye that sizes up the swell by day, the other shining in the night...

'Well,' says Delphine, mightily pleased, a figure now unique and bright: 'China? America? Which is it to be?' and Goran says she'd be wasted there, on either one.

She says, ‘I’d quite exclude America for now – the place is growing back to where it was before the Italians discovered it and made it kitsch. It’s back to nature now ...’

‘Where would the Italians go?’ asks Goran. ‘This must be your fantasy.’

Delphine says, ‘O, they went to China, mostly; and the armies, well, they ended like the buffaloes and those passenger pigeons, down in the hole. The other guys all went back home and – I guess – they lived much happier there for almost ever after.’

‘Well,’ says Melinda, ‘That’s half the story. Don’t believe a word. China is more interesting. But after all, we’ll have the party first.’

‘Good!’ Melinda says to Delphine – ‘You’ve got your party body on.’

Delphine’s new lion face – is just too close to mine, a tic, this peering, or perhaps it’s something more: she speaks as if she’s shovelling down her words into your mouth, a trace of gin and onion too.

‘She’s just what Goran wants,’ says Niobe. ‘Though to be left like this – when one is dumped, there’s sadness, even jealousy.’

‘Party, party – come on, you guys, enjoy yourselves,’ Melinda shouts. ‘There’s not a storm in sight. Start with the conversation, that is how it’s done, the fun comes in the second act,' and here's Niobe, and she tells me of her father, drunk, her mother shrew, and siblings spilling out. I say,

'Niobe – why d'you tell me this? It's trivial, why do you think it's worth telling and remembering?' She cries a little, then she says it's all she can remember, that's her conversation, and I say, 'Well, all the worse for you,' and turn away. Delphine is new, to be explored, but Niobe – just all worn-out stuff …

Delphine says, 'I always thought you guys were rather crap – the job, all that, and fluid loyalties. Those warring states, in China all split up – they have Parties there – they're not like these that we shall have,' and I'm annoyed, and tell her of my box. She's not impressed. I say, 'We're angels now. We see the men and women scamper round, but – we have no voice – we use our wings to dry the routine tear.' She turns away, and says, 'No fear! I'll go where I am sent, I'll tell you everything.'

Melinda says, 'I think we know your story, dear. It's pizza, and the written language for the Mongols riding through,' and Delphine says no, no, she'll really go, and tell us all. We've done great things, of that she's sure, and worth some flattering.

I stand alone and rocklike, until Goran says to me,

'You spoil the party thus. Forget your Africa – I'll have a word, we'll give you cash, Melinda will. We'll make a park – the big guys you're afraid of: they will be the cops, the farmers will be conservationists. The guys from Xinjiang, they'll come for holidays and pay the bills. There, that's your Africa resolved, let's hear no more of it,' and I am pleased, I guess, though maybe unemployed again.

Delphine reminds us once again – the written language, Mongols – where did those end up, they couldn't all have gone back home? and Goran says maybe they'll etch upon his wall 'Here at the start, and at the last,' it's not quite true, but it will do – and in the gloom that falls we wish there had been a Mr Sticks to drum us through, or even Mister Kite with drugs.

'Come on, you guys,' Melinda shouts, 'five for a party isn't good – it's better just with two, or lots for orgies – let's make do, meanwhile, with conversation...'

I say to Niobe, 'When we found you, were you there for warmth or stealing?' and she starts to say 'a bit of both', and that is trivial too, when Delphine says,

'You guys – erase America from your thoughts. You won't have heard a lot from there in recent months – and that's because: it's empty now!'

Melinda scoffs, 'No no, they've just dissolved a bit,' and Delphine says,

'No, no, they've almost all gone home. The Indians went to Xinjiang – they'll find a place, it's twice as big as France, the others back to where they came from: even those Italians, who discovered it and settled first.'

We've heard her say it all before, but now it seems it's really over for them now, those Americans, and Goran says, 'There! That's a ripe fruit of Intelligence – you see, Delphine is on the inside track. Besides, we Macedonians had done it all before those Yanks – empire, democracy and perpetual war – those were our signature goods, and now we scarcely have a home. America: the only thing I'll miss – those shapely autos: for a while they had the fantasy, big cars, big people stretching out,' but Niobe again – those tears! – she weeps and says,

'The food! The secret's surely lost,' but Delphine says just wait a bit – 'you'd trip to see the canyons empty as the moon, the prairies infinite, the animals just wandering up and down, the buildings wrecked and taller than Persepolis – such wonders! Deserts now deserted, no more gas and restrooms – no more "hustle, hustle", no more hustlers – the baseball averages congealed, stuck there forever, yes, it's truly dreamland,' and look! her eyes! the red one warning, and the white that penetrates the night –

'Maybe, my dear,' Melinda says. 'You'll tone that body down, when you are off in Xinjiang, you must blend in, you know,' and Delphine says she's happy that the Africans can stay back home, forget that history, stay and be guardians of the parks, although I think that maybe in the end it's animals that have it all, can be protected, eat each other under tutelage, and multiply as best they can.

'You see,' Melinda tells Niobe, 'it's all to do with grasping the connections: capital, money, work. If you don't read the book, the world falls down.'

'I quite see that,' Niobe says. 'But book there was, and is, so why...?'

'It didn't say what guys had hoped to hear,' Melinda says. 'They did one thing, so quite unlikely they would want to do another thing.'

*

Goran says, 'They played me like a fish, a little fish. Melinda did it all, the plot. They kept on putting me on trial, always acquitting me. It wears you down. That's why we took the bus. They catch you and they let you go, and on it goes: your mouth gets sore from hooks.'

'Well,' says Delphine. 'What are you going to do about it? Jump out the water – if you are a wise and active fish, that's what you do.'

'Ho hum,' says Goran. 'Not that easy – just ask him,' he points at me, but I am cured, my feet can carry me to India, and far beyond, and even swim to Surabaya, where I've always hoped to live and die – a beach house, and the sound of clarinets ...

‘You fool,’ Melinda shouts. ‘Goran has schemes that fail – but you’re quite passive. I accomplish! This job is – doing what you want. You,’ she shakes her claw at me, ‘you’re a reactionary, that’s the truth of it.’

I say, ‘It’s just I come to things from quite another angle ...’ and there’s Niobe’s face, it swings from one to other of us, like a lantern on a tree.

Melinda says to her, ‘Don’t be wistful, it is all to come,’ and Niobe says, ‘They’ve told me how it’s going to be and how I’ve missed the best of times. At least I’m not a monster like you’ve made Delphine,’ and Goran says Delphine will be presentable when she goes off, her quest; we’ll put her on the bus – and then I feel the fear, the fear of something gripping me, it holds me down, some octopus – its arms, or having frondy fingers grope you, they suck you in, you’re small – in you go, it’s darkness in the dark, you’re in some wispy thing, maybe a stripy shell that trundles, you can suffocate there in the sea, even if you are a fish....

Melinda shakes me, and she says – a box, a horse, a ship, they’re all the same, you move around in them, they’re moving too, just lighten up, enjoy the travel, if you can. Goran deserves far more than he has got, like she’d deserved Niobe, and if not her – Delphine.

We wave Delphine goodbye.

*

How do you tell, if China's ruled by seven warlords? Like in the opera, with pheasant feathers in pouches on their backs, and wispy facial hair? Delphine will know – she's an academic.

'Our Party was a flop, maybe the same in China,' Goran says.

We go inside our beach house: ringed with cactus, Melinda's aerial on the roof. She practises her fiddling. It's not at all like Surabaya.

Delphine – the figurehead, new mermaid at my prow. Some future there with her for me, perhaps?

And here she comes! My, that is wonderful. So quick! Some swift analysis ...?

'No, no,' she says. 'They tossed me off the bus. I vomited.'

Melinda laughs. 'You fucking humans! Of course, I get messages off my aerial, but ... we need explorers, everywhere,' and she points at me. 'Go! It is your destiny. America. Then China. Go!'

Delphine says her gut's been tampered with, it's something Goran must have learnt when fighting in his war. Melinda says Delphine will wait and stand there on the shore when I get back, or if she's still nauseous, then maybe Niobe ... they're not enthused with me, but Niobe tells us she's learned to twirl, and Melinda says to me,

'We've fixed your Africa, unless they try to sell it off again.' I don't much care for voyaging, nor coming home, I don't anticipate I'll find the meaning of our lives but – what comes after this modernity, yes, that is interesting, would be something new, that doesn't feature in the epics.

And I stroll a little way along the road....

The road to China passes through America

There's cactus everywhere. There's no sound of cajun fiddle – the Acadians, the cajuns, have left that continent. Melinda's trying out the Chinese fiddle now – it needs to be attacked, with vigour, quite surprising. She's deeply into cultural stuff, she doesn't need to read the books, remember names, or hum along. We've struggled, to trail along behind her, as she goes further, further into culture – into the midst, the heart, those shrieks and scrapes of fiddling.

She's fainter now. 'How China's ruled America – is empty. Concentrate – that's all it takes, to find another place.'. That's what's to know. America – is empty. Concentrate – that's all it takes, to find another place. Forget the sentiments and rules – though those must come in, I guess – though never knowable without a wrestling in your mind, a limning constant of ideas implanted, stuck there, from way back. Forget the nursery instructions, – where are the rulers now?

The CYBERIACAFE. 'Hey,' says this guy, Yen, 'We're all a ways from home in here, some exiles, some just running. I can call you Zhu,' he hugs me, I resist – this guy could come from half the world. I'm irritated, and I say, 'I've got a quite good name ...'

He says, 'I can tell you all about China, and I'll take you there. And you need a name, so's they know who you are. But it's all useless if you have no history.' It seems an innocent thing, and so I say,

'Back there, there's Niobe – she's beautiful, but ...'

'Then not for you,' says Yen.

'I don't want her – it's just her beauty, I want to spoon it off like jam ...' I say.

'Where'd you think to spread it?' he asks.

'I don't know.' I say: 'She divines ...' and he interrupts – 'In China almost everyone does that.'

'It's best there's just one oracle, so it simplifies. Then, there's Delphine – she could be my guide, only her guts play up.' I say: 'She'll guide the ship – it takes no skill, she's painted, fixed. Niobe spins....'

'That's quite decisive, then,' says Yen.

'There's Goran, he dumps women who're too young,' I say. 'It's his atonement.'

'He must have qualities,' says Yen.

'I fear that's so. Passion, adventure,' I improvise.

'That leaves you sounding rather dull,' says Yen.

'I haven't started yet. There is Melinda – our Valkyr,' I say. 'She makes the new designs, that change the world. Then someone rubs them out. She starts again. Which brings me back to China.'

'Come with me. I'll show you,' says Mister Yen. 'All.'

Fearing a kidnap, I ask him, 'Why should you do so generous a thing?'

'It helps me put the things in order. The journey is not to start the ending, the return, but to find the honest man,' he says. 'The rest's just crawling spiderlike upon the globe. Not setting things as they were, then back you settle in, a scarred and tedious man, hero returned and pooped. It's – finding honesty. Then, you can die.'

I'm almost without words. I say, 'I hope to find new men, new women, with new views on what men are, and women too. After us, we narcissists, there's sure to be a new morality, new expectations – new but distant boundaries....'

His eyes shine in anticipation: there are tears as well. He says, 'I hope that too, but maybe you already know what you will find. That's sometimes the best way.'

I tell him, 'Surely there are wise guys there – the books say so – the question is, if I can siphon up that wisdom, bring it home and profit from ...'

He says, 'I'm sure you can,' quickly, and quite kindly.

'Where'd we get the horses?' I ask. 'Not from Kazakhs – they squeeze your hand until they get their price.'

'Camels?' asks Yen. 'But if you're out impressing women, the beauties even, you'll be looking stately on a camel, that's for sure, but you're too high up, those women – they can't share your dreams.'

I say, 'The bus is unpredictable, an aeroplane may drop.'

Yen says, 'We'll work on it, the transport angle.'

I wonder if I'll find just narcissism, all over China; though instead of worries and desires quite disparate – like we have here. They say they'll focus on a few dull things. Family, enormous wealth, green marble mausolea ... A motto for the wall comes to my mind – "All that matters is not honesty", or else, "What matters isn't honesty". The trouble is, a wall that's meant to be an epitaph, and not keep people in or out – it should be unambiguous. That is the job of walls, they say.

Yen says, 'Your mind is racing over wider fields, it's like a hare. You'll need more cash. I'll manage it for you.'

In the café, he introduces lots of other guys. There's lots of them who manage cash.

They're from all over, these young thin guys, with names that do not fit the language on their shirts.

Yen says, 'That Delphine – into guiding. There's business there. People who tell you where you are and where to go.'

'Maybe, yes,' I say.

'Niobe – she spins?' he asks. 'Well, spinning's in a lot of cultures, but ...'

'It's just a thing that people learn,' I say, and then, 'There's Chinese opera, of course – we have our fiddler, and there's Niobe, she is agile, the weight no disadvantage,' and Yen says,

'Hohum. There's not a lot of business there. But – in this voyage, remember, you must accept just everyone, even me, even your friends – exactly as they are. Not take offence. Not damage as you pass.'

'The communists,' says Yen. 'They only thought about the people. That was a big mistake. Demanding, too. Now, there is more.'

'Animals? I say, hopefully. 'My guys live by caring for them. As for the revolution, culture, back and forth – we talked about those things, of course, Goran and I – it never did us harm.'

'Lights,' says Yen. 'Bags of neon. And mist, like the prints, with dust below and brilliance above. Those mounts eternal – horses, camels too. Dignitaries, lots of those. Many Americans, many in command.'

The café's full of Indians, from every nation in America: it fills, it empties out, they take survival packs, food for a week, and go to Xinjiang.

'Maybe we shouldn't think of riding animals,' I say.

'No, no,' says Yen. 'They like it. That way they get fed. Besides, some smaller ones – they taste delicious,' and he thrusts a finger in his cheek and twists it to show pleasure extreme, and great discernment: the rarer animals are under glass, and you can see them roam about and pee on trees.'

'You must tell me more,' I say.

'Then, there's the invisible hand,' he says. 'It puts you where you build the house, the office and the bridge. Then you do it. All of that.'

'Yes, yes,' I say, 'I've been it, that invisible hand. It's policy. But if the things fall down, or don't get done?'

'In China, there's been dragons from the start, the mischievous things: the wrangle for the pearl, on boats, processions – sewn on your pyjamas Uniting heaven with the earth.... It's just – they are not eats,' Yen says and laughs. 'They're tame.'

'I mean,' I say, 'the rules, how they are made. Disobedience. The jails. The palace.'

He stares at me: 'You're just a tourist. I hope you won't offend.'

He goes on, 'Poor people – they are being phased right out, however long it takes. They are not wanted.'

I say, 'New order? New boundaries? Cognition and image? Warlords – would that be a step back, Yen?'

'Back?' he says. 'More human. Prickly too.'

I say, 'No one knows if it's that to come,' and he smiles at me: says,

'You find out in the office, when you have to go.' He goes on,

'When I was – am – there – there's a law of physics, as you'll see: that things extremely small, are fuzzy, indeterminate. They live in a state that experts call "a storm". The storm, it could be start or finish,' and he goes on. I do not listen, but I say,

'I'd no idea.'

He says, 'It's true you could split up the land, the mass, in seven pieces, but remember – the same river runs through all of them. It's just its colour changes – yellow, blue, and green, and black. And brown and pink – and red, at the last, discharging in the sea, with all the stuff tossed in....'

'I can't wait,' I say.

Yen says, 'Impatience! If you return to Niobe, how long would you think you'll have to be together?' And there's a tear of reminiscence glistening on his tarnished cheek. I say,

'A minute – that's how long it takes to sink encounters deep inside,' and then he says,

'Before you leave – the guys insist: a little ceremony!'

When you go voyaging, bizarre things come your way, and not just tempests – here they are, the guys from the café, camel drivers, and they lift me up ... In triumph! No! They toss me high, and there I see, behind the wall, whose characters I can't make out – there's many alphabets in play – the plains, the desert, monks, accountants, many, many Indians and – 'Are those buffaloes?' I shout.

'No, no,' the camel drivers cry, and down and up I go, below the sweaty heads, beyond – that pictogram, does it say 'welcome all', or 'welcome wall'? Anyway, there's guys that's climbing up and over, no one comes the other way. And then I'm down.

'Now, you're a camel driver!' What a shout!

I say to Yen, 'I haven't got a camel – it is transport that I need.' He says,

That Mister Kite – he goes much higher still than you, and gave the guys some cash, and drove his camels fast, and my! What songs he sang!'

There's the beach, and there's our house. I've trudged the long hot road. China – another day, another camel'.

Behind us all – there might be Mister Kite, his cash, and his evasiveness – for sure we need both now

Here's Delphine: I ask, 'Where's Niobe?'

She's irritated, 'That's not how you should return at all, from the sea you'd come, borne on a high wave, with tales and spells, and vengeance, setting all to rights. Niobe's gone – there was a spat – with Melinda. And a spit – for Goran. She's off to look for guys, I guess. That's what the people do.'

I think, 'Fuck Mister Kite, and all his cash. He took the transport, paid on the nail….'

'Well,' Melinda says, 'You're quite useless in relationships.'

'It's understanding what they're for,' I say, quite weakly. 'I can't quite fathom them. Maybe Niobe did good to seek some destiny.'

'For sure yours wasn't China,' Melinda says, sharply. 'Is there a Lenin there? Or someone else, not so stubborn, and closer to us in time? A pattern? Some purpose? An intelligence? Some helmsman?' and at that she laughs.

'Those things – they didn't occur to me,' I say. 'I don't know how you'd find them.

She's dissatisfied, she says, 'If you're a liberal, you're in exactly the wrong job.' I say,

'I'm interested in the inner life – of how guys might react to some design, and how the picture changes, colours appear ...' and she shouts,

'Well! There were some decent guys, those camel drivers, with their games and songs. You could have quizzed them! Besides, the soul's a thing you need to have, if you're inclined that way, but looking for the details of it – well, you'd waste your time. The guys there – are they rich on other people's debts, or poor on theirs? Or vice versa?'

I say I'd like a wooden house to live in; outside, a persimmon; maybe rowans, and she says I'm old and rotting meat, you live in what there is, that other guys have bust themselves to build – if you don't like, there are the fields and being woken by the cops – you take your choice ... and on she goes.

Delphine says she's glad to be with Goran now. She should be our guide and figurehead, though it is true the prow goes only where you point it, and she says that Goran made her over, gave her this new look, forget the travel, and I say – 'It will not last,' and she says that she is glad for that.

I tell Goran that the wall says 'welcome'.

'Walls don't welcome,' Goran says. 'Why not just write "wall" upon it, not be boastful calling it "Great Wall". A human word upon inhuman bricks or other stuff.' And then he sees the word is quite inhuman too, it's inorganic – maybe that's the point, though why he wants that humans leave a print is ever more obscure. 'It's not a mark, it's just a message, to be read from space,' he says. 'Or by the dinosaurs or creeping things that come hereafter,' and I say,

'Well, that's your project, Goran, so rejoice! You've found a thing that does no harm,' and then I see outside – a guy. He's surely one who caught me, put me in my box – I run, and find a piece of something, maybe some armour fallen off a tank, a weight of fifteen kilos, shaped like a frozen shoulder of a cow – and when I think of shoulder, frozen, in my mind there comes the boy at school who sat beside, he had a frozen neck, and when he spoke he turned to you, twisted his whole trunk as if in politeness exquisite, painful too.

*

I hit the guy – he doesn't ask my motive, so I'm sure he's the right one, my persecutor. I hit some more, he's reeling now, he's no defence, I club and club. He doesn't bleed, he dents, and when he staggers, there! I hit some more, and more, to excess and have him done and finished with.

He falls into a kind of trench that stops the sea, or helps spring run-off – I won't look, or examine him, I let him lie.

Delphine says, 'What a performance!' Goran nods and nods.

Melinda asks, ‘Someone explain?’ but doesn’t wait for answers.

‘Where’s that goddam Mister Kite,’ she shouts: ‘I’m waiting for his secrets now!’

‘Goran got involved in other people’s freedom,’ Delphine says, proudly, forgetting Mister Kite, his cash, his pills.

‘It’s surely always so,’ says Goran: he is irritated. ‘Your own liberation, you can manage that at home. I’d just the problem, that those other people were another nation. So they said. It interferes. But that’s quite usual too.’

Delphine persists: ‘Those Macedonians – it’s all inherited. Brought civilisation, almost reached to India. Freedom and civilisation’s almost quite the same,’ and he’s more irritated still, and says:

‘Delphine – it wasn’t civilisation, it was styles and boundaries. Walls, like the one we’ll lay down on the ground, to show we came and went,’ and he looks round for help that Delphine doesn’t give.

‘You exaggerated, Goran,’ says Melinda: ‘That’s where all the trouble comes. You didn’t make the right friends, and you took it out on enemies too vigorously,’ and Goran says,

‘Take it out? Melinda, what does that mean to you?’

‘You know quite well, Goran,’ says Melinda. ‘You push things with discretion, you can shove, but there’s trouble if you club,' and so she looks at me, as if my trouble's bound to come. She says, 'Delphine, you're quite a clever girl, but you,' she points at me, 'Mister Zhu! As we must call you now – you're not a genius though you're the service of the intellect: pack up and do, that's what the genius spirit says – you, you pack up, you don't do. Look what a mess you made of Africa. Scared of the guys, of taking part: you didn't see the sunsets, didn't take your magic stick and dance. Didn't hunt and didn't plant. Now, they're all keepers in a zoo,' and on she goes. It's true. And Goran nods and nods.

*

Look, look at the darkness coming!' says Melinda gleefully. She thrusts her great beak at us, clacking like a stork. 'Poor Niobe! Let's hope she has found port!'

'Executions in the bath,' Goran reads out from a paper. 'That's a terrible thing, though it does keep you clean. It's French in origin, this use of standing water: the legend says they didn't bathe.'

'We must stop it,' Delphine says. 'Everything that I'm against.' She wrings her hands.

'All will settle down, you'll see,' says Melinda, comforting her. 'People can't stand things, some guys fight back – what do you expect? Mister Zhu!' she laughs. 'No one's suffering where you come from, except some animals, and they have every chance to reproduce and fill the gaps.'

'All the amusing people have gone quiet, their fun is stilled,' says Delphine. 'They used to break the rules and joke and eat too much. Minds brilliant too, the best of educations ...'

'Their money's gone, is all,' says Melinda briskly. 'Besides, Delphine, with your digestion, dear, you'd never stand an evening with the fancy crowd. The aristos. Now, I guess they work out in the gym,' and up and down she jumps, to show, and sings a woodbird's tralala.

The storm! It's back again!

So's Niobe.

She says, 'Yes, I think in a new way – it's just I can't express, by standing still.' Melinda says, 'That's natural,' you see she's torn between not having had Niobe, and now not having Delphine.

'Where I was,' Niobe says. 'I was with some Russian guys. They fought for me, and some – they wore mascara….'

Melinda interrupts, 'Yes, yes – you were there – in China! That's for sure. In China!'

'Well,' Niobe says, 'It's not that different from if you're not. Guys fight for you – it's in their genes.

Mister Kite was there – he has a business now – selling big black birds to eat.'

'Everything is different there,' Goran says.

'But no!' Niobe says, 'that Mister Yen, who guards the wall, he says they've all got what they want, no need for communism now,' and Goran mutters that there's something more than that, but it's all gone by, so what's the use, and Niobe tells us of the lights, the singing until dawn and then the exercises, wherever she has been; the *frites*, fried chicken too, and Melinda says it's heaven but ...

The storm. The executions, guys on the run and hiding round the corners – 'I just have to know,' Melinda says. 'Where's next?'

The storm sails in on its black wings.

'We need that party,' Melinda shouts, 'Niobe's back, the sly-boots. Then – batten in, enjoy the storm!'

'O no,' Delphine says, 'No more of Goran's making over – I don't lead, just go where I am pointed, these parties make me stiffen up.'

Melinda says, 'The point is going where you're pointed – I keep you guys, I get some other guy to pay for you exactly so's you can be useful,' and Niobe says, 'Of course, each on her own is just a twig, and you're the branch, Melinda,' but I think of rooks – of twigs that go into the nest: they don't make flowers.

'I can't ask,' cries Melinda. 'People! They don't know! Look, look, the people – running, running every way! So far, so fast – it's not the poor, they walk and stick, it's peoples, whole ones ... What do they seek? – it must be something, not banal, not some crap job, not tenderness, and not return to some forgotten wife, blood on the tapestries, things as they were, they are. It's not like there's a Trojan war, for nothing – some bird-woman; coming home, vengeance and then order, that war's over, justice fudged – now, just imagine! – they run from wars, to wars, wars significant and valuable, towards whatever comes, wherever there's a space, and then away again.'

Goran whispers that it's she who makes it so, it's not the wars, it's the money and the flags that start them off, and she says he's superficial, and it was liberation and some ground to put his hut on that got him where he is now: in trouble.

And so the party starts. Again.

Melinda tells me, 'You're a mediocre human being, but your writing, the literature, there is your salvation! Not people – literature, policy, there's your gift!'

'If it's truths we're after,' Goran says, 'Niobe is short, fat, adolescent, fixed on Russians. As for oracling – a seer that's worth his fee is blinded as he peers through holes in his foretelling stone. Gets burnt live, there on the beach. A tar barrel does the trick. That's not foretold!'

And he laughs.

'This will be a short party,' Niobe says, and that is true, storm pressure punches in the window panes, the sand comes in, and then the sea.

'Stop, stop!' screams Melinda – 'My string, my strings – they'll get soaked! You idiots! – not a wall, Goran – if you can build a wall that's prone, you can surely make it be a bridge, and get us safe and dry, over to the other side – see! it rises like a rainbow ...'

I say, 'Melinda, this is the sea. A bridge will be no use,' but she has taken lymph, lymph and youth flow from the storm, she waves her fiddle like a spear, and cries, 'You, Mister Zhu, will play the hero's part, and lead us where the sun shines always, the fruit tastes of play and innocence. Here, take my fiddle, for once attack it like a man. I'll even find a drummer – no, no one shall be sacrificed, not one of us to calm the waves, not even Niobe! Let's go across this skyline bridge to empty lands, and populate them with fresh giants and dwarves ...'

We stare at her. The house is full of water, it shifts about, masts lost, it creaks – those archways, based, I think, on the Alhambra's, lean to the left and then to the right.

'She's brewed the storm and something else to put on top,' says Delphine, gagging as if her acids boil.

'Mister Yen!' Melinda says. 'He is the key, the key is his. I'll summon him, he knows the polities in China, how to reach them. He is the chancellor, the keeper of the gates,' and on she goes.

'He rents, rents camels,' Goran says, but she insists, it's transport, essential, you know exactly where it goes.

*

Mister Yen. She summons him. The beach house leaks out in the waves. 'Hmmm,' says Mister Yen. 'Bad scene in heaven, then?' and laughs.

Melinda, in a haughty mood, says, 'Mister Yen, some lessons on the violin I'll beg from you for free. That is our secret. But – what I need from you's the truth. Tell me, in detail, and in characters as tall and firm as you can brush – what we shall find beyond your guardhouse.'

Mister Yen thinks long, and says, 'The trouble with our violin, is I don't know how it ought to sound. The thing is, not to scare the camels,' so, they start to speak of politics.

*

'We could take boat, escape,' I say.

'No!' Goran says. 'Melinda pays us. We're her cabinet. Of curiosities. But – she makes things happen, and she tweaks.'

'She only tweaks where things are going, where they want to go,' Delphine says.

'We could go to your animals,' Niobe proposes, 'They only eat each other, their lives are valuable to us, more to us than to themselves.'

'It's just another exploitation,' Delphine says, 'All the rest goes on – these are house slaves. Their life ends in the sand, not the killing pit, is all.'

'Well, you're the moralist,' says Goran, quite nastily. 'And better so. Not guide, but preacher!'

'Ha!' says Delphine. 'So, Goran, you had a higher purpose when you liberated guys who didn't want? Ethnic liberalism, that's your song ...'

I say, 'Let's build this goddam wall, and lay it down. Forget the boats, the animals – there will the storm. We're Melinda's cabinet for sure – but not to govern anyone. We amuse ourselves; straight faces, though.'

Mister Yen says, 'Better to have a trade, even a poor one, than to rely on begging ...'

Delphine says to Yen, 'All those people moving in and filling up the sandy space – do you have good lives for each and all?'

Niobe says, 'That's no fun and jokes. Good lives are a bore,' and Mister Yen snaps at her,

'Spin, my angel, spin.'

Delphine says, 'No wall, no bridge – if I'm a preacher, then I want like in the mosque a pulpit reaching way into the congregation, into their ears and hearts,' and Goran pops Delphine's breast back in its brocade, hoists up her tunic, maybe the collar's spiked. 'There, Fido,' Goran says. 'You are a guard dog now.'

We are convinced there's much to say, orders to follow, disobey, but there's too many other thoughts… Niobe says,

'Yes, build the goddam wall, and leave the message. Sum it all up, and move us on to other things.'

A slogan? 'Come to China,' Mister Yen suggests.

Goran says he wouldn't think of going there, much doubt remains. He'll do a stint with Delphine now, he says. Maybe it won't please her, but he'll be all the better after it.

Along the shore we hear a sound like cracking twigs. Melinda's drummer, trying out: 'Keep time, keep fucking time, you creep,' she screams. 'My time! Listen!'

Way down the beach – we hear singing, maybe Chinese singing, but not opera – more beautiful than mermaids, or those sirens.

Delphine says, 'Melinda's got it right! Her poetry…. That is perfection. Or then again, it is her ambition that unlocks the gift,' and in the pause that follows, there's the drummer – a shaman's drum, with infinite discretion pattering. I see he's got two paddles, like they use on cimbalons.

Delphine says that Goran's her first convert, but he must renounce his sins, and those of all the rest who come to mind.

He's quick to dump the past, he says that socialism was the punishment they all deserved for what they'd do in wartime, and I say, 'Goran, that's grotesque, though maybe true,' but we don't start the argument. He says,

'Delphine, now we must find a church for you to stand on and surround you. Then we'll kit you out with some beliefs. For now, the tone's what matters, charisma, reaching out, all that.'

The singing pours into our ears like paradise, so free, so disciplined, up like a lark, down like bejewelled toads. It breaks off, and we hear Melinda crow,

'The innocents, the innocents! now we must save the innocents!'

It is a warning for us, and I say to Niobe, 'Bring the ship round here, and we'll be off – the other shore ...' and then, 'O no, Niobe, this is no ship, this is a boat, and scarcely that. A rowboat! A dory!'

'That is what they had,' she says. 'The epic warriors…' and sits down in the back. I take the oars, they're like two trees, we breach the wave – one oar points up, the other sinks, the water's like cement. And then she calls, 'Vassily, come o come – Vassily, come!' And here they are – a congregation, noses like empty bottles in the waves: the dolphins.

'Here's the dolphins, they will help us,' says Niobe. 'You, Mister Zhu – that was your specialty, to know them all by name, protecting them ...' and on she goes. How beautiful, she lounges there, she twines her arms, the lovely snakes, around some bits of wood that's maybe seats, and cries,

'Row on, row on, the dolphin host escorts us to the other side, and there we'll found an empire, or at least a colony ...' but no, we're driven back upon the beach.

Of course.

'The innocents,' Melinda shouts. 'Now they await us – I've awoken them from centuries of boring sleep!' And so we're back with her and her designs.

'Abandon ship, brave sailor,' shouts Niobe, she's laughing at me, and that row of raptor's teeth, they make me angry just to look – I say, 'It's destiny, Niobe, neither joke or tragedy,' and at that she laughs and laughs.

'You did nothing to ensure good luck,' she says, 'No rites. And so ... of course! It's destiny for sure.'

Melinda sings and sings, and 'Thank you, Mister Yen,' she shouts, 'For teaching me the culture,' then – 'I love parades! Stilts! I'm in heaven.'

She says for sure, his country isn't broken, besides, not her responsibility – it's like a meal that comes in seven parts, the courses are just separate by nature, there is tea and rice, and fish, and all the rest. Rivers and caravans ... and Mister Yen says not to expect too much, the nomads go by train these days, but she is drunk with it, and after all, , prepare for the surprise. America came to its end and stopped, it's done, it went no further, nothing to do but all go home....

'This mad bird, what does she want?' asks Mister Yen. He says, 'And Goran – what's with this religion? Sending out Delphine, a mission.... Why should we care?'

'For sure,' I say. 'It's his remorse. Atrocities, no doubt. Things done and not, beliefs indigestible and so thrown up. Religion's just his box of chocolates – Delphine, though, she's the picture on the top. She's Goran's supreme priest. You seldom get to eat the picture – that's his game,' and I'm smug, I've taken my revenge on him, on Delphine – my burial's avenged.

I am at peace.

'Melinda?' I say. 'She wants to be the chief. One of your kingdoms – that's why she sings the songs.'

'Hmmm,' says Mister Yen. 'I think I'll keep her out of there. She has no qualification, that's for sure, for being queen, and empress.'

'She summons up the storms,' I say. 'Flies with the birds. Feeds on the corpses too.'

'Well,' says Mister Yen. 'It could be worse – some big ideas, mind changeable – but all the same....'

He thinks deeply: 'Well, we do have a kind of vacancy ...'

Melinda rushes up: 'How do I get in? I didn't learn the singing just for fun. Jobs won – perhaps by individual combat?' she asks eagerly.

Niobe seems enthusiastic, and I suggest, 'Those oracle bones? Do they attract, await?'

'No, no,' Niobe says. 'The clothes. And woven cushion covers.'

'You're not the kind who makes a nest, my dear,' Melinda says, quite kindly.

Goran says there'd be some room for Delphine's church. 'Not spirituality, but friends and social climbing,' and Delphine says, 'More likely country club, line dancing.'

Melinda ignores them, and she asks me, 'Where would you fit in? I'd need my counsellors, of course. Not you! The literature – you could do all that.'

I say, 'I had in mind a mountain, if there's any left, I see myself up there, a sage, quite inaccessible to most, but full of silent wisdom.'

Miser Yen looks glum: 'The lady, Melinda – she'd need consensus. And no hurricanes. It's good she has no principles, and lives by song, not cash. She has but little nourishment for spirits, but her terrifying aspect – it always helps.'

He turns to me, 'Now, Mister Zhu, share your slow infrequent thoughts with me. China's the coming thing, that's clear, and everyone is setting up their shop or tent – the fabric creaks, it crumbles, but it holds, it always has. This Melinda, though – she could wreck it all. To start her off, lessening the shock when she appears – she could be called Ma Lin; the cultural shift is slight,' and on his cool pragmatic way he goes. I say,

'She is a monster. Ambition. Pride. Indifference,' and Mister Yen starts laughing, 'Yes, yes,' he cries. 'That is exactly what we could expect. I'll put her on the list.'

*

'We can't go with her,' Goran says. 'Nor can we let her go. Melinda's time with us is up. Now, I can't do the deed, my hands are soiled. It's your turn, brother – Mister Zhu! Pure and noble though you are ...' and on he goes.

I say, 'It's true that if we go, I lose my date with destiny, the ship, the waves, the monsters – and temptation too! I hate to lose temptation – and you, dear Goran, you would never see the sea again, never to come to – wherever you might call home. But – assassination? Of Melinda, who we know, alas, too well…?'

'You do it this way,' Goran whispers, 'Take the lead-rope. Round the neck, a foot quite firmly in the back, and pull. I've seen it done so many times,' he pauses, disavows. 'In the movies, naturally.'

Then Delphine says it's all free choice in there, and she's a mind to take the colours that they use and found religion on it, and we say the idea's as good as any that's been had – the yellow and the blue and red, and maybe white and purple too, yes, yes, a whole theology is there ... She lets us off a capital charge, maybe: and we're relieved.…

Niobe too is keen to go – she says to me,

'You're just the sneaky type, without much character – but you're so tranquil, perhaps – riding down the trail with you –' but then she shakes her snakes, the camels snort and bubble at the sight, and all is stormy for a while.

'I'll tie my drum here, on this hump, for when ...' the drummer says. Melinda sees him, and she shouts, 'No, no, forget the hump, I'm dumping you. There's plenty of your colleagues there, we don't need you.'

The drummer says at least she ought to pay, and she cries out, 'Pay, pay? Yours is a gift, like baldness or red hair. You can't expect some pay for what all have inside,' and she shoots off a tralala to show. The drummer says, 'But ... but ...'

She interrupts – 'Ut? Ut? Yes, that denotes the key of C, and shows that what you've got is international, a universal tongue, so when the aliens come and gaze on Goran's wall and wonder what it means, you could be there to greet, and set the time: your skins and paddles – beat the beat!' she cries. 'But not right now!'

'Mister Yen,' she turns to him. 'Not everyone that goes to where I go can enter by this gap, hole in the wall.... It is to Yuxi that we go – ah! see the colours! Drumming! ... Distant drums, the thunder....'

Mister Yen says, 'Do you know how far that is? Yuxi! The miles, the rivers, deserts, mountains too,' and he begins to weep – 'My camels! Have you thought of them, my dears, my assets,' and she interrupts:

'Well, there's the rent,' and Mister Yen says, 'Yes, there is a kind of rent,' we buy the animals now, then if we bring some back, he'll refund some cash. 'But,' he says, 'the people there – they've laboured and they've suffered, and the suffering goes on. Maybe they seek a rest from guys like you? You bring more storms, that is your gift, that's why you're here...' but she insists, this is no time for prejudice – it's enterprise, a foreign woman's maybe what they need, she folds herself round Mister Yen, she yearns, she wheedles; but, oh his unavailing tears, heartbreaking –

'Do it, do it now,' Goran says to me. 'Courage, Mister Zhu. Get it over with, kill her, kill Melinda, awful crone – then back to sea for me, you to your ghastly ship', and there is Niobe, sprawling in the sand – 'These goddam beasts', she says, 'Mine stands before I can sit on,' so I say,

'You've got the good one. Give it me, at once.'

Now Goran sees our murderous plan recede again. He says,

'The motto, for the wall – it's nearly perfect, just it needs a little pith. I thought, maybe, "The sea, the sea!" but maybe that's obscure, it means you always find what you've been looking for, though if you have no ship, it doesn't help.'

I say, 'Sea wall? Or wall of sea? Merely a slogan? – must it be seen from other galaxies? "The wall, it falls before the storm" comes to my mind. The wisdom's there, but not the pith. Maybe more thought should be bestowed, dear Goran...? Caution, prudence….'

And then, Melinda calls.

She calls, a shriek, no tralala; now, she's the bird of wisdom – not at dusk, but at the dawn. She shouts, 'O Mister Kite, o hear us,' then to us she says, 'He'll scout the route, he'll be our guide; his birds, his whistling owls, white eagles – augurs in the sky – will go before. He speaks the language camels speak, he has the pills for happiness, forgetfulness – he has the rank … he can't be seen, let's hope he hasn't perished in the storm …

'And now, we must perform the good luck rites,' and here's Niobe, dancing round some flames, I think I hear her chant, 'The war, the war,' or it might be Goran's motif: 'Wall, the wall!' No gods show up: a spin or two – those feet, those boots... perfection – enough, enough!

EPILOGUE

There is no turning back: Melinda summons us, and she must be obeyed. We can't resist. We drop our destinies and run to join the caravan. Melinda's at the head, she waves a kind of spear, and Goran says to me,

'You idiot! They should have left you in your box, it's thanks to you, our moment's passed,' and Mister Yen has waved us through, he hugs each animal 'farewell', his tears abound – sitting up here, it's like we're rooks upon a mast, a tree that sweeps the sky. The guys pour out from the CYBERIA, they cheer and laugh. We leave the one steppe, and here's another steppe, and Delphine says, 'the journey of a thousand miles starts with a single step'...

We laugh.

Melinda says our journey is a longer one by far than just a thousand miles. We face the front, no one will come after us, but now she's called, our fate is fixed, another story opens up before us all….

Niobe says to me, 'I'll ride beside, you mustn't touch me, though,' and I reply I hadn't thought to, being the tranquil kind myself….

So, on we ride.
To China!

About the author

John Fraser has lived in Rome since 1980. Previously, he worked in England and Canada.

www.ingramcontent.com/pod-product-compliance
Lightning Source LLC
Chambersburg PA
CBHW020547310726
48979CB00008B/1125/J
* 9 7 8 0 9 5 7 2 0 6 1 0 6 *